PARTY GIRLS

PARTY GIRLS

short stories by Diane Goodman

Autumn House Press

PITTSBURGH

"Autumn House" and "Autumn House Press" are registered trademarks owned by
Autumn House Press, a nonprofit corporation whose mission is the publication and
promotion of poetry and other fine literature.

Autumn House Press Staff

Editor-in-Chief and Founder: Michael Simms
Executive Director: Richard St. John
Co-Founder: Eva-Maria Simms
Managing Editor: Adrienne Block
Community Outreach Director: Michael Wurster
Fiction Editors: Sharon Dilworth, John Fried, Stewart O'Nan
Associate Editors: Ziggy Edwards, Erik Rosen, Rebecca King
Designers: Kathy Boykowycz, Chiquita Babb, Rebecca King
Media Consultant: Jan Beatty
Publishing Consultant: Peter Oresick
Technology Consultant: Evan Oare
Tech Crew Chief: Michael Milberger
Interns: D. Gilson, Caroline Tanski

PENNSYLVANIA
COUNCIL
ON THE

ARTS

Autumn House Press receives state arts funding support through a grant from the
Pennsylvania Council on the Arts, a state agency founded by the Commonwealth of
Pennsylvania and the National Endowment for the Arts, a federal agency.

ISBN: 978-1-932870-52-7

Library of Congress Control Number:

All Autumn House books are printed on acid-free paper and meet
the international standards of permanent books intended for
purchase by libraries.

Blessed sister, holy mother, spirit of the fountain, spirit of the garden,
Suffer us not to mock ourselves with falsehood
Teach us to care and not to care
Teach us to sit still.

T.S. Eliot, **Ash Wednesday**

Contents

PARTY GIRLS

Beloved Child

I know Aiko is frying the bacon in her wok, using chopsticks to turn the pieces without even looking at them thanks to her inherited skill and grace. Not a drop of grease would dare splatter upon her. Gil is in charge of lettuce, lovingly wiping down each leaf with a wet paper towel as if he were bathing a newborn child. He also keeps his eye on the wheat toast browning in the toaster oven. Donny is in his BarcaLounger in the living room, reading some impenetrable book, underlining passages key to him which he will quote during lunch. He is puffing on an unlit pipe.

I am not there yet but I know it is exactly as I imagine it, this preparation of our Saturday "family" lunch. Aiko had said "Avocado BLTs" so I said I would bring the avocado and the tomatoes, as soon as I finished my long swim at the university pool. Aiko had said "no, no, I can get them" with that odd urgency I never quite understand when I offer to help. But I'd insisted because if I bring nothing to the Saturday lunch, then I am nothing but a guest.

Normally when I am swimming, I am pleasantly lost and not thinking. That's why I swim in the pool instead of in the ocean because the ocean has no walls to turn me back and I need the freedom of turning back. In the pool, Bruce Springsteen sings in my head. But today, thanks to Veronica Smiley, I was thinking about why Gil's desk isn't covered with pages for the draft of his book on Thoreau. It is summer and Gil is an assistant professor at University of Miami; he spends his summers writing this book, which he hopes will find a publisher before he comes up for tenure. He has three more years. In the locker room today, Veronica—Gil's department Chair—asked me how his book was coming and it occurred to me that I didn't know. It also occurred to me that I didn't care because if I cared I would probably know but then what propelled me through the water was trying to figure out why I didn't know. I seem to care about that.

It is nearly noon when I get home and I am almost late so I run up the stairs, taking two at a time, breathing in the gorgeous smoke of bacon. I undress in my kitchen, throw my wet tank suit into the sink and slip on the t-shirt and shorts I'd draped over a kitchen chair before I left. I grab two tomatoes and put them in a bowl with the avocado I'd left to ripen on the windowsill for just this occasion, and a lemon. I am starving. My hair is wet and tangled and I smell like chlorine.

Donny is a very large imposing man but no one ever calls him Don or Donald. He has a buzz hair cut, a goatee and one pierced ear, in which he wears a small silver cross although he claims not to be religious. He is thirty-five years old and does not have to work. Aiko and Donny have been married for over five years. They met six years ago at the University library, when Donny was a graduate student and Aiko worked at the circulation desk so she could take dance classes for free.

Donny keeps most of his past a mystery and all Gil and I know is that his parents died in a hotel fire somewhere in Europe while he was here writing a dissertation on T.S. Eliot. When he inherited their fortune, he quit school and, shortly after, married Aiko. He is an only child. So is Aiko. Gil has an older sister named Loretta. She is paralyzed, in a wheelchair, and lives with Gil's mother, RuthAnn, in Phoenix. I have never met them.

We all live in the house Donny owns in Coral Gables: Aiko and Donny downstairs, Gil and I upstairs. Donny continues to educate himself and thinks we are his students. Gil teaches Freshman Composition, an introduction to literature course, and one section of his specialty, 19th century American Literature, where he gets to spend some time talking about Thoreau. Gil loves to be outside. He and Aiko take lots of long walks around the campus when I am at work and Donny is either reading or taking his afternoon nap. They "commune" with nature, they say, loving its "grandeur" and its "sadness" and "yet its hope." They use these words and phrases not as if everyone does but to point out that everyone does not. Donny does not seem to hear them, and usually I just plug Bruce Springsteen back into my head. I tend to gravitate toward "Born to Run" at these times and there's no irony in this.

I love to swim. I love the power of my body when it moves through the water, the small satisfying breaths, the pushing toward something and the return, pushing and returning, freedom with boundaries. I would do little but swim and cook if I didn't have other obligations. Aiko still takes dance classes at the University and she takes care of Donny. She is Japanese-American, slim and sturdy, delicate but not the porcelain doll you would expect. She is freckled, especially across the bridge of her upturned nose, and she has gleaming blue-black hair that is cut in layers to her shoulders with bangs that are always just casually touching her almond eyes. She has a deep voice that is a surprise coming from such a heartbreakingly beautiful girl. Her mother still lives somewhere in Japan. Aiko talks about her mother often, about how she misses her. When this happens, Gil nods in complicity and often says 'I understand. It's the same for me. Phoenix can be as far away as Japan' and I turn my face away so I can roll my eyes as Aiko says, 'I know,' because it is not the same at all. Phoenix is a four hour plane ride away from Miami. In the three years that Gil and I have been together, he has never gone to visit his mother and sister. Not once. But he loves to suffer their absence.

Suffering absence is what binds Gil and Aiko, what suspends them above the ordinary world.

I go downstairs and walk into Donny and Aiko's part of the house without knocking as is our way and pass Donny reading in the lounger. I say hello. He reads, *"in my beginning is my end"* and I say "that sounds right" and go into the kitchen, into the scene I imagined, and also into the heavy quiet leftover from last Saturday's lunch. Gil has laid all the washed leaf lettuce out on clean paper towels and is going for the toast. Aiko is blotting the perfect bacon. I go to the sink to wash my tomatoes. No one says hello, not even me, but then Gil asks, "how was your swim?"

"Wet," I say, and, angry at myself for saying it, turn on the water. I wish Gil wasn't so handsome; it makes me angry and more sarcastic than I want to be. Lately, his whole being has become unbearable. He has a perfectly sculpted face, like a model's, with the strong jaw, the high cheekbones, the dark blue eyes and naturally pale, almost see-through, skin. His teeth are perfect. He has straight blonde hair that he is always pushing off his forehead, a gesture that was for a time endearing. He wears huge square tortoise shell glasses that he really needs and which make him even more handsome and more unbearably so because on someone else they would look ridiculous. He has cultivated this look of eternal sadness, even when he's smiling. It makes me sick.

Gil and Aiko are close friends, much closer than Donny and I are but it's necessary to all of us: Gil is an empty receptacle that I could never fill and so I am relieved that he and Aiko have the kind of relationship that lets them feed off each other's never-ending grief: they are both the children of dead minister fathers. Sometimes their sorrow can be trying, often annoying, but at least I have a career which provides hours of escape. Donny is home almost all the time but he is not interested in the constant amorphous sadness that permeates the rarefied air Gil and Aiko breathe; in fact, somehow he doesn't even seem to notice how bound up they are in their shared melancholy.

Whatever is going on now has been going on for a while, or at least for a week. At last Saturday's lunch, tuna melts on rye, I looked over at Aiko while she was laying the farmhouse cheddar slices onto the open face sandwiches, while Gil was holding open the broiler door, and saw she was crying. I said, "Aiko, what's wrong?" and she said "My father was a minister" and then I said "I know" because we all knew that and then I said, "so was Gil's" which was something else we all knew but that they both always loved to hear. In Japanese, Aiko's name means *beloved child*. It was the name her father gave her.

That day I had brought a homemade lemon remoulade I'd mixed with dill and capers; we were going to spread it on the rye before the scoops of tuna went down. But, as usual, I was almost late and Gil and Aiko had gone ahead and assembled the sandwiches before I got there. I'd said, "Oh, but what about this remoulade" and immediately Aiko went to the refrigerator and produced a lovely platter of crudités that she had prepared earlier.

"So you knew I'd be late?" I said.

4

"I didn't want your spread to go to waste," she answered, in a low small voice that said she was clearly upset about something but whatever it was, no matter how grave, she was still thinking of me.

That kind of sacrifice is pure Aiko; family first, her own troubles later. She had a way of relaxing her grief so that it made room for more timely obligations that needed to be fulfilled, like laundry, bill paying, or slicing vegetables for remoulade. Aiko's father died seven years ago, Gil's eleven, but they both live in the wake of those deaths as if they had just discovered them. Before he met Aiko, Gil kept his grief going through a career in literature which provided endless opportunities for personal sadness and Aiko, I imagine, nurtured hers out of honor and private necessity. But then they found each other and their friendship took their combined sadness to an entirely new level, one that made them almost happy. But I was so tired of being confronted with all that old sadness all the time so I stuck a carrot into my remoulade and put it in my mouth so I did not have to inquire any further. By the time Donny came in from the living room and started quoting from Robert Frost, Aiko's tears had gone away.

Today Aiko asks me if I want her to slice the avocado that I am in the process of slicing. The kitchen is not small but it is small enough for all of us to see what each one is doing. I rub a cut lemon on the slices so they won't turn brown. Then I add some salt and pepper. I say nothing because she is not expecting a response. She knows the answer but she can't help herself. I begin to slice the tomato and it spurts all over my t-shirt, seeds and juice. I am the executive chef at the South Miami Country Club. I have to be at work by 2:00. I am always covered in food.

Aiko and Gil instituted our Saturday lunches two years ago, a few weeks after Gil and I moved in upstairs. They won't let me cook anything for the lunches, and wouldn't even let me help if I didn't insist on doing something. They say I shouldn't have to do the work I do at work in my own home.

I met Gil three years ago when his department hired the country club to cater their Christmas event. I stopped by on my way to work to check on the catering staff and Gil was there early too because he was in charge of drinks. He had pitchers of iced tea, and bottles of wine coolers and beer that he had put warm into a silver serving bin. I saw him struggling with the ice and walked over; I took the big bag, threw it on the ground three times to break up the cubes, and then poured the ice over the warm bottles. Gil was not embarrassed by what he called my expertise; he was grateful and relieved. He said, "Wow. You're small but really strong" and I said, "Not a big deal. I have to do this stuff all the time" and we got to talking and before I could leave, he'd asked me out for the next night. I said yes because Gil was handsome, because I had the next night off, and because I had been in Miami for going on two years and had not met anyone other than the staff at the country club. Not that I'd had any opportunities to make friends. I lived in a room off the kitchen at the club, and I swam in their pool at 6:00 am before the members arrived. The rest of the time, I tested recipes, met with vendors, supervised the budget, oversaw the parties, and cooked. The country club was a stepping stone for me; I had just finished culinary school when I took the job and believed I'd be moving on to another place in another city at the end of three years. Living at the club allowed me to save the money I would need to really launch my cooking career.

On our third date, Gil took me to a very dark restaurant for dinner where the hostess and the waiters knew him by name. He rented a room in a house in Coconut Grove and didn't have a kitchen, which didn't matter since he didn't cook, and he ate nearly all his dinners in this place. By the time our entrees were served, I knew a lot about him: the story of his dead father, his disabled sister, his suffering mother who lived far away in Arizona. I knew he played tennis, loved the Miami Dolphins and why he'd gravitated toward Thoreau. In the candlelight, he was beautiful and his sorrow was seductive and I stayed with him that night in the single twin bed in his small room. It was summer in Miami and the air conditioner was old and weak but when I woke up in the morning, I was freezing. It only took a few seconds for me to realize that I was freezing because at some point between sex and waking, Gil had wet the bed. While I was trying to gracefully wiggle out of his embrace, he woke and immediately started crying. I know for some women, all of this—the pee and the tears—would be a deal breaker but it wasn't for me because I peed in swimming pools all the time and assumed everyone else did, too, and when Gil held me very tightly, seemingly unaware of how his embrace forced me deeper into the wet sheets, and thanked me over and over again for understanding, for being who I was, I immediately absorbed the idea that I was a person who could rise above someone else's humiliation, who could understand.

6

And now I hear Aiko thanking me for the avocado and tomatoes, as if I'd brought them to her as a gift. I ignore her, as we assemble the BLTs. Aiko has torn basil into the mayonnaise, a trick she learned from me. Gil spreads it on the toast and then adds the clean lettuce. I lay the tomatoes down, then the avocado; Aiko adds the bacon, a bit more basil mayo, closes the sandwiches and slices them through with a Ginsu knife. She calls Donny in for lunch and he lumbers to the table with his book, lifting a large bag of potato chips from the top of the fridge that only he and I will eat.

"My father loved bacon. He would eat it on almost anything. On Sundays, he would put a scoop of vanilla ice cream on a waffle and top it with maple syrup and crumbled bacon. And then I would do it just because he had done it. Like father, like daughter. His beloved child. His illness lasted too long," Aiko says. I am certain that she and Gil talk about their fathers every Saturday while they are preparing our lunch and that it is the remnants of their memories that darken the kitchen by the time lunch is served. Perhaps this new bolder sense of dread in the kitchen is just the product of deeper and more personal exchange. Usually Gil will follow Aiko's inevitable comment about her father with one about his own but today he just sits there, staring at his sandwich on the plate.

But then Aiko picks hers up to take a bite and Gil does the same. Aiko eats in the most irresistible way, half perfunctory and half passionately, and both aspects of her eating have a profound effect on me. Between culinary school in France and trying to make a name for myself through the country club restaurant, I have tasted nearly everything only to discover that while I have a sophisticated and sensitive palate, there are a lot of foods I don't especially like to eat. But I always want to eat everything Aiko is eating just because of the way she eats it, even unusual Japanese delicacies her mother sends that smell like dead fish or wet mud or eggs gone bad. I am certain that even though Aiko and I are eating the exact same sandwich, hers tastes so much better than my own.

"What do you think it was that God could have been thinking?" Aiko asks.

"*In his end was his beginning,*" Donny says, paraphrasing from the book, which is open on the table in front of him. He passes me the chips. I take three, stack them up one on top of the other, place a piece of bacon that fell out of my sandwich on top, and bite.

"I ask myself that all the time," Gil says, ignoring Donny and responding to Aiko, "it's excruciating." I didn't really hear him say this last line because of the extraordinarily loud crunching in my head but I'd heard him say it so many times before that I recognized it by the way his mouth moved and how his shoulders slumped. And by the way both he and Aiko lowered the sandwiches they held in two hands into their laps and then lowered their eyes. The adult children of dead ministers, they were grieving.

I slam one of my bare feet onto the other, hard, to punish myself for thinking that, and try to remember that there was a time when I truly, genuinely, felt Gil's loss and wanted to try and fill it. But I cannot make those memories return to me so I change the subject.

"So Donny, what are you reading?" I ask.

"Rereading. *Four Quartets*. Eliot. So if everything leads to the present, to this moment, pointing to now, what is the beginning? Everything, right? Everything is the beginning. Every second. Aiko's father's death, Gil's father's death, their lives, these BLTs, all of it." He polishes off his sandwich and begins to look around for another. Aiko has one ready on the counter behind her and spins the top half of her body around like the dancer she is or was meant to be, lifts it, and spins back to put it on his plate.

I wonder why Donny does not include his own dead parents in that litany but then I begin to understand. He does not want his sorrow to be present. Satisfied by my own deduction, I celebrate by taking a big bite of my sandwich and a slice of avocado slips out and joins the tomato spots already on my t-shirt. Aiko jumps up as if I am on fire.

"Club soda," she says, heading to her frig.

"Old shirt," I say, "don't bother," but bothering about others is what Aiko does best so now she is pouring the soda onto my shirt and rubbing at the green stain with a paper towel. I am thinking it would be good for her to have a child, someone she could take care of who, unlike Donny, would respond to her constant need to care.

"Excruciating," Gil says, again, as if we had all sat silently since the first time he said it. "He had to pee all the time, or at least he felt like he did. But he couldn't. So he would moan, and then scream for hours until the doctors gave him something to make him pass out. I did not understand what God could have been thinking."

"In his end was his beginning," Donny says, "like a baby. Wailing. Help-less. Waiting. Peeing. Aiko, a beer?"

"Yes," she says, rubbing the last of the avocado out of my shirt.

Even though I don't want her to be wiping my shirt, even though the shirt is old and thin and I would be happy to throw it away, I am helpless to stop her. Silently, I am wailing and waiting and hoping that my end is not in my beginning because if Donny and T.S. Eliot are right and the beginning is the present, then my beginning is right now here in this house in Miami and I do not want it all to end here. At least not here, in this kitchen, at the family lunch. I do not want this to be the rest of my life.

I look at Gil and see that his sandwich is still in his lap and he is nodding his head, as if he is agreeing with Donny, or Eliot. Or just having one of those conversations that he often has with himself. I stare at him, will him to look at me. I know he knows I am waiting but he will not look up. If Aiko looked at him, I think his head would snap up so fast it might go flying off his shoul-ders. I think I see a drop of spit fall from his lips onto his lap but then I real-ize it is a tear. I want to slap him.

When Gil and I met, he had been friends with Donny through the Eng-lish department; although Gil was a new assistant professor and Donny was a grad student, they were the same age and gravitated toward each other quickly. Gil had not met Aiko, though; he'd just heard Donny talk about her, about her beauty and her homemaking, her easy happiness and her obedience. "She sounds like a paper doll," Gil had told me. He said he was surprised that Donny would have such an old-fashioned wife, someone so young who was so content to just take care of him. Gil said he was lucky to have me, someone with a career, with ambitions and a sense of humor. I was pretty sure Gil didn't "have" me but I liked him fine and living with him had given me a life outside of work that I had little trouble getting used to. In the beginning of our relationship, despite the periodic crying jags, we had the kind of excitement and fun all new couples have, everything we did—from movies to dinners to bike rides on Key Biscayne—seemed as though we had invented it, our sex life was sweet, on my nights off, we watched videos until the early morning and before going to sleep, had breakfast in bed. We didn't seem to notice our life together morph-ing into routine but I like routine and I like order; plus, I wasn't home very much because of my work schedule and when I was, it was easy to hold Gil, to have sex, to tell him everything was going to be all right. It made me feel good to have someone other than my country club staff depend on me. Gil believed me and that made me feel good, too; it made me happy to know that I had the kind of power to lift away sadness, that with just a few words and the pressure of my hands on Gil's back, I could make things better. And I thought everything would be all right: I was young, twenty-seven, but even so I'd had enough life to know that every bad or sad thing that happened to you was not the last thing that would happen to you. I was living proof.

We had been living in the room Gil rented for nearly a year when Donny offered us the first floor of his house and we went there for a drink, to see the place and discuss the possibilities. Aiko set down a tray with flutes of champagne and sushi she'd rolled herself and told me she'd had a dream about me before she even met me and she put her hand on my knee and squeezed, perhaps to make sure I was real. She said she knew I would be coming to her before I ever appeared, that we were meant to be family. I don't usually trust that kind of hocus pocus but I was moved by what I thought was her sincerity; plus, at that time, I thought she was this caged wife who needed a friend.

A week after we moved in, Gil came upstairs from having helped Aiko bring in her weekly load of groceries. He had stayed to help her prepare a dinner they would be eating that night while I was at work and he said he had been wrong about her. She wasn't just this young passive girl living in the dark ages. She was more than that. She had depth. Her father had also been a minister. He understood her.

Now I seem to be the one not understanding much but instead of slapping Gil for crying in the middle of our "family" lunch, I thank Aiko for laundering my t-shirt and stand up to do the dishes but Aiko reads my mind and says no. It is not so hard to read my mind because the same thing happens every Saturday: I stand up to do the dishes and Aiko says no. Now Gil has stood up and is at the sink running the hot water, having barely touched his lunch. Donny is back in his book, asking what's for dessert.

Last month was Aiko and Donny's five year anniversary. I insisted they celebrate it by having dinner at the country club. Of course Gil would join them and it seemed less pathetic of him to be with them on their anniversary if I was at least partially there. Plus, I wanted to cook a family meal.

I planned a special five course dinner, things that are not on our menu, and I meant to cook it all by myself while my sous chef managed our dinner rush. I started with a seared foie gras, drizzled with a balsamic reduction, finished with pink peppercorns and warm blackberries. I came out shortly after it had been served. Donny's plate was empty, wiped clean with some of our homemade French bread. Aiko had taken one bite and Gil had taken none— he was moving the berries around his plate, coating them completely with the reduction.

The first thing I said was, "Hey, I thought this was supposed to be an anniversary celebration," but other than Donny nodding his head in agreement, no one said anything so then I said, "Oh, I'm sorry! I should have thought about the foie gras. Not everyone likes it," except I knew Gil loved it and I'd seen Aiko eat way more controversial food than goose liver. But she said, "No, it's lovely. It's not that," but she did not say what it was so I nodded my head and went to the kitchen to prepare the salad.

I tossed microgreens with a fig vinaigrette and then topped each salad with crispy pancetta and a poached quail egg. When I appeared at the end of that course, it was the same scenario. So then if it's not the food, what is it? I was about to say but the folks at Table 26 began applauding when they saw me.

"This carrot-ginger soup, it's gorgeous," a woman in a white sheath dress said.

I smiled a grateful thank you.

"You are a wonder," her companion stated, still clapping.

I let the sous chef and the line cooks finish preparing the anniversary meal and I stopped going out to check. Aiko always carried with her white cards that had her name and phone number embossed in blue; she sent one back at the end of the evening but I was pan-frying snapper with one hand and flipping a pan of baby vegetables with the other so the waiter stuck the card into my apron pocket.

When I got home that night of the anniversary dinner, Gil was not there. I knew he'd fallen asleep on Donny and Aiko's couch, as he often did when I was working. I knew Aiko had covered him with an afghan she had crocheted. I undressed and then remembered Aiko's card in my pocket.

It said, "you ARE a wonder and we love you."

Who loved me, I mused, stretching out alone in our king size bed and hoping for a long dreamless sleep. Donny liked me well enough, thought I was funny, but dismissed me in the way he dismissed everyone—with patience and some good humor. To Donny, we were all sort of necessary impediments to his private literary search for truth. But Donny liked having an audience, and a home and a schedule; he liked to eat and drink and be around people when he wasn't reading. I suspect he also liked having sex with his beautiful wife but about that I was not entirely sure: they never touched, displayed affection, shared inside jokes. I didn't see any passion there, which didn't necessarily mean there wasn't any passion there, except anyone could see the passion Donny had for books. He loved reading. And he loved talking about what he was reading to the people who were around. I was pretty sure he loved his dead parents and that he did not love talking about them. In that way, I understood him.

Gil loved me with a kind of relief I grew accustomed to. He needed a lover, and that I could be, but he also needed a mother, a protector, a sympathetic ear and although it was easy enough for me to go through these motions, I did not care for him the way he imagined I did because I did not want to love anyone in the way Gil imagined love should be. But that is what made us such a great match: immersed in literature, Gil made assumptions and presumptions about how my actions translated into what he wanted to believe I must be feeling; he embraced his theories as truths and they made him feel superior and sure. My knowing this had the same effect on me and so we coexisted peacefully. I was not demanding in any way because I did not need much. I kept his secrets and didn't chide him or flinch when he cried, wet the bed, stayed silent for days on end. I knew he trusted me and could explain away my vague detachment through his interpretations and my clear presence, which he believed was a sign of devotion.

Aiko loved me because she dreamed me, because I was evidence of her powers. And because she believed she had created me, she could turn me into anything she wanted me to be at any time. That's what made me a wonder.

At today's lunch, though, I am wondering what I am supposed to be. Aiko and I are going through our usual tug-of-war about the dishes but I am missing something. Something new. I can feel it.

"Don't worry about the dishes," Aiko says to me, as she does faithfully every Saturday, "you need to get ready for work." Gil is soaping up the sponge; he's already filled the wok with water. Aiko has given Donny a stack of Oreos which could only mean that she did not have time to bake and that makes me suspicious.

"What did you do this morning?" I ask, because she always bakes on Saturday mornings so we have something homemade for dessert after lunch.

"I had an appointment," she says. "Do you want some Oreos?"

"No, thanks," I say, "an appointment for what?" I am slight and bony and love any kind of dessert more than just about anything else so my refusal and my follow-up question make everything even more awkward and uncomfortable.

Aiko puts the package of cookies down and looks at me.

"Let's have it," I say, because now we both know that I know something is going on but she just shakes her head and looks down. Gil is washing the dishes in water so hot that I can see the steam rising off his wet hands and I know they are burning. There is pain in those hands for sure.

Donny eats two Oreos at a time and asks if there's any milk. Or, better yet, he says, can someone make coffee?

"Anyone can make coffee," I say, and walk toward the kitchen door. "I have to get ready for work."

"*Go, go, go, said the bird: human kind / Cannot bear very much reality,*" Donny reads.

"Amen to that," I say, and leave.

Suddenly I realize that I have been waiting for a sign. I have been waiting for something or someone to tell me it's time to pack up and go, to leave the country club and move on. Maybe to New York. To work with the real chefs— Mario Batali, Bobby Flay, maybe even Eric Ripert. I have proven myself at the country club but I need to know more. I need real instruction, real inspiration. And mostly now I know for sure that I need to get away from Gil, and from Aiko. I think today's lunch is my sign: something is happening and I realize that it's something I don't want to know, not because it would hurt me but because I sense impending drama that I do not want to witness. I want out and when I say it out loud—*I want out*—all my anger and frustration seems to fade away. I get into the shower and think that tomorrow, before I go to work, I will work on my resume. I start humming some Bruce Springsteen, this time *Sherry Darling*, and this time out loud, not just in my head.

When I am dressed in my chef whites and nearly ready to go, I hear Gil coming up the stairs to our part of the house and I think I am fine, happy in fact, so I start to go to the bedroom door to greet him but then immediately find myself back in the bathroom and closing the door. I turn on the hair dryer, even though I have already dried my hair. I hardly need to start sweating now, before I get to work and the real sweat behind the line will begin, but I do not want to listen to Gil now. If the sound of his footsteps could make me retreat, then I know the sight of him will bring back all the bad feelings my epiphany and shower just washed away, which would make all the good feelings I just had not real. Maybe I do want to know what's happening with Gil and Aiko? Except that I think I don't. And yet, I feel as though I want to murder someone.

I know he is sitting on our bed and hope that he will get tired of waiting for me and go back downstairs. I turn off the hair dryer and wait for a few minutes. I hear nothing and am relieved. When I emerge from the bathroom, my head hot and sweat coming down my hairline and sliding into my ears, he is still sitting on our bed with his hands folded in his lap and his eyes downcast. Same as it was before, except without the sandwich.

"I'm sorry," he says.

"For what?" I ask, and sure enough, my anger is so palpable I think I must have a fever.

He looks at me as if I should know the answer and then looks down into his lap again.

"I am sorry about all these downcast eyes," I say, trying to make a joke that even I don't find funny.

"I don't know how to explain...I'm sorry. It's just that Aiko and I, only we really..."

"Hmmm, must be lonely for you two," I say, and then because suddenly I am about to implode, "in The Dead Ministers' Children's Club."

Either Gil is not fazed by my nastiness or he does not hear me. "Yes," he says, and when I don't respond, "this is excruciating" and I feel the avocado

BLT threatening to come up, and then he says, "I'm sorry. I wish I could make you understand." But I do understand. Perfectly. Gil and Aiko have made a pact to dwell in a cave no one else can enter. They are the children of dead fathers who were ministers and the shelter of their grief protects them, makes them smug. I get it.

I say, "I'm late," even though I'm not, and I leave.

I drive to the country club fuming but not really knowing what exactly is bothering me. This is my way out. I should be relieved. And I am because I am tired of Aiko and her sanctimony. I am bored with Donny. And I do not love Gil. So maybe I feel guilty about lying, about pretending, and maybe that is what is bothering me so much. In our first year together, when we lived in his small rented room and were getting to know each other, Gil and I spent time talking about our pasts, our families, our fears, the things we said we had not told anyone else ever; as I got to know Gil better, I knew he had probably told lots of people his secrets but I had been telling the truth. Then I was done talking and wanted him to be done, too. I wanted to move on, to live in the present, in the now. I was very busy with work and when I was off, I wanted to swim, go to the movies, the beach, drive down to the Keys, go to restaurants and have great chefs cook for us, drink wine, watch the sunset. I wanted to ride bikes, plant flowers on the little balcony off the room, listen to music, play cards. I wanted to have fun. By the time I realized that Gil wanted none of these things, that he only wanted to keep talking about his past, his father, his sister—or he wanted to read and then talk about the way what he was reading related to his past, his father, his sister—I was so tired, I didn't have the energy to leave him, to find myself another apartment or a new guy. It was just easier to stay.

"No matter how much you talk about the past," I had said, "it stays the same. You just hurt yourself." I knew a lot about this: my mother died when I was fifteen. But it didn't matter: I had been a teenager and she was a single mother—not a minister father—so it didn't count. When I told Gil, I left out the details; I thought death was enough. But it was not. To Gil, my grief seemed thin and without punch, almost silly. He probably didn't even tell Aiko.

Reservations in the dining room are full for tonight so when I get into the kitchen, I call a meeting to see what kinds of specials we can offer that can be prepared quickly and will last for the whole service. Normally, I already know what kinds of specials I want to serve—this is my kitchen and ultimately the responsibility for all the dishes falls on me and that's how I like it, how it must be. This kitchen is my child: I conceived it, created it. I take care of it and devote all of my passion to tending to it, nurturing it, making sure it is the best it can be. But tonight, like even the best parent, I am weary and distracted.

Tao suggests something braised, a spicy pulled pork over polenta that can sit on the stovetop all night and just be ready to go, and I say yes right away and send him off to prepare it. Harriet, my sous chef, asks if we can do a pasta entrée special, something like gnocci in lemon with asparagus and olives. Harriet makes the most glorious gnocci. Beautiful, I say, and she goes off to make the dough. She is smiling and I realize that my staff, too, are like my children, even though many of them are older than I am. But it is my job, my responsibility, to guide them while making sure they can be confident on their own. I hand-picked them when I started here and despite the difference in our ages and levels of experience, we grew into this kitchen together. I can be tough and I can be critical but mostly I think I am loyal and supportive. I know I am as proud of them and what we do together as I can be.

I think that two specials might be enough for tonight when our intern, shy Marie, blurts out that the Ahi looks beautiful and asks if she can create an upscale entrée-size salad with it and when I say yes without even thinking, she literally runs into the prep kitchen before she thinks I have a chance to change my mind.

I have frightened her, though I am not sure why. I thought my enthusiasm was obvious, but she ran away. I wonder how Marie sees me and then it occurs to me that I don't know how Aiko or Donny or even Gil perceive me now, other than as someone who doesn't understand. Donny would never presume that I could understand the books he reads or the things he says; to him, I'm the cook who lives upstairs with his old colleague, the professor. I know Gil perceives me as someone who is not Aiko, someone who cannot understand the significance of the past. And Aiko? She must perceive me as an extension of herself, since she thinks she created me, the part of her she thankfully does not have to be. So it seems as though there is a lot I do understand and yet I am not convinced.

Dinner service goes smoothly despite the big crowd and the Ahi salad runs out after twenty orders because it is such a big hit. Marie approaches me timidly at the end of the service and apologizes: she is so sorry she ran out of the special. I tell her don't be silly—everyone loved it—and then she thanks me. For trusting her. For my faith in her. I see her arms moving toward me, like she wants to reinforce her gratitude through a hug, but then she must think better of it and puts her hands in her apron pockets fast.

"What don't I understand?" I blurt out, and she literally recoils.

Marie is small and shy and very young. She has an obvious fear of authority so I think that even if I was on my knees and kissing her feet, she would still be afraid of me. Perhaps more. She is the wrong person to be asking this question to but everyone else is busy shutting the kitchen down and I need an answer now.

"This isn't a trick, Marie, honestly. I just need to know: is there something I'm not getting?"

She says, "Chef, I'm sorry, but, uh, I don't know what you're talking about," and her lips are quivering.

"Do you trust me, enough to tell me what's going on?" I don't think it's that Gil or Aiko don't trust me. I think it's more that they have a secret that they want to keep to themselves.

"Nothing's going on," she stammers, "I'm sorry, Chef."

"Sorry about what?" I say. What was Gil so sorry about, sitting on our bed with his hands in his lap? What is there to be sorry for this time? What are the people I am with everyday doing that they keep apologizing to me for? "Tell me what you're sorry about." My voice is thick and dark and rising.

"Um, well, I don't know," she says, and I see her struggling to figure out how to say what she thinks I want to hear. She loves her internship, is hoping it will turn into a full-time job when she finishes culinary school. She does not want to get fired. And although she could not know this now, I love having her here and have no intention of firing her. I am living in two worlds, the one where I am battering a fragile cook who has made a fantastic salad tonight, and the one where no one will tell me a truth I realize now I desperately want to know.

"Tell me the truth," I say. "Just blurt it out."

"This is your kitchen, Chef. And you're a genius. Everyone thinks so. I am so lucky to be here. But tonight was . . . different. Weird. Because normally you don't talk much to us, you don't really need to, I guess. I mean you need us, yes, you do, but it's also like you don't. You're quiet, you're concentrating. Everyone always says that you're in your own world, but in a good way, you know? But by yourself so we were just surprised that you needed us to help. To help you. That you asked us for help."

I never saw this coming. Or what came after it.

"Thank you, Marie," I say because I need to put her out of her misery, "the salad really was gorgeous. We're going to run it as a special all summer. We're going to call it *Marie's Summer Ahi Salad.*"

"Oh my gosh, thank you Chef," she says, and I think she might faint. "Thank you so much, I don't know what to say."

"Great, go on now, help the others shut the kitchen down," and she literally skips off like a child.

One morning when I was fifteen, I got up to go to school, just like every other morning. My mother was in the kitchen with her nurse's uniform on; she sat at the table with me drinking herbal tea while I ate my toast and told me that today she would not be able to drive me to school. She said she had an early meeting at the hospital and I would have to take the bus. Sometimes I took the bus, and my best friend Allison and I would chew as much gum as we could before we got to school and had to spit it out so taking the bus was fine with me. My mother walked me to the door and pulled on the lapels on my jacket. She said I was a good girl, which was something I already knew, and kissed me goodbye three times, which was our habit. Then I walked to the bus. When I got home, around 3:00, there were two cars in my driveway: my Aunt Sue's and a police cruiser. My mother's bedroom door was closed and when I went toward it, the police officer gently pulled me back because my aunt was crying too hard to stand up.

My mother had crushed a bottle of Valium into her morning tea and then got back into her bed to die. After that something important shut down in me. But I didn't know what I no longer had, what had vanished along with my mother, and I have never told anyone the truth about this.

When I get home, I am surprised to see Gil in our bed. He is reading. It's nearly three in the morning. When he sees me, he puts the book on his lap and takes his glasses off. He has no shirt on and his chest is milky white, like an old man's. I can see some of his veins and I wonder if he is completely naked under the covers. I stand at the end of the bed and stare at him for a couple of seconds, trying to figure out which one of the things in my head I want to let out first:

I understand.

Here is the truth.

What on earth is going on?

But before I choose one, he says, "Aiko is pregnant."

I am sorry.

Here is the truth.

Is that what all this fuss is about?

"Wow," I hear myself say. "Wow. That's great. When is she due?"

"Around Christmas."

"Boy or girl?"

"We don't know yet."

"Oh. Oh, boy." I take off my chef whites and the sweaty bra and panties beneath them.

Gil is staring at me, though not at my nakedness.

"They'll be great parents, Donny and Aiko," I say. "Here's to the next Beloved Child."

"You don't understand," Gil says.

"I'm going to take a quick shower," I say, which is true because I am heading into the bathroom, and then, "I'll be right back," but that part is a lie because I am already gone.

Abracadabra

The restaurant is crazy busy and my entire head is engulfed in the heat and steam and smell of all the dishes being cooked and readied on the line. I am tired. I am always tired but this is where I like to be. Where I belong. Everything seems to be as it always is but when I look up from the trout I am just about done sautéing and see someone I don't recognize standing where the servers stand while waiting to pick up their orders, I think I am hallucinating.

He is young, maybe thirty, slight, not smiling. But his lips are parted and his teeth—very white—are clenched down in a hard bite. He is too handsome. There is menace in the way he is looking at me.

"You need some help," he says.

I am thinking the same thing. I need some help, I should call out for some help, because despite the kitchen heat my skin is cold and I know the hairs standing up on the back of my neck have nothing to do with the kind of fear I normally have when I am feeling threatened. This is something else.

But maybe I am dreaming. God knows I am exhausted and no one notices anything is amiss. Waiters use their hips to back him out of the way as they reach for plates and he disappears but then like a wave, he rolls back up after they've gone. I close my eyes, open them fast and there he is. I want to swallow but my breath is in the way.

"You need help," he repeats, morphing through the steam this time into a lost boy, his forehead the kind you want to brush hair off of.

I hear myself say, "I don't know, do I need help?" and when it comes out it sounds like flirting. Someone is flirting with this stranger-boy on my line in the middle of my dinner rush. The trout is overcooked, beyond saving.

His face relaxes then. "You look like you do," he says.

There have been some things I wish I'd had the prescience to understand before acting on and when I remember them, I want to set myself on fire. But right now time is moving too fast for memory to intrude. When I don't answer, he says, "I put in an application for a cook. Your ad said you needed some help." That is true. Then he looks around the madhouse that is my kitchen and says, again, "You look like you need help."

What do I look like? It has been so long since I have thought about it, since I was pretty. I have been sweating behind the line for two hours, for too many years, and sweat makes my small face wet and a bright red. At the end of every dinner shift, when I go into the employee bathroom at midnight to splash cold water on my face, I find my morning mascara, that small homage to vanity, has left my lashes and settled into the deep cups of skin beneath my eyes. I am forty-five years old, always bone-tired yet plagued with nervousness all the time, even when I sleep. I am married to my South Beach restaurant, entering it in the dark mornings and leaving it in the darker nights so I never see what I am supposed to look like, the public I might be compared to were I ever to put myself among them. I hardly see the daylight. I wear chef whites every day, stained with grease and sauce. I know exactly what I look like and feel surprised, and then ashamed, that I am so sorry about it right now.

"Why did you do that?" I ask him. It is the next morning and he is here to fill out the paperwork.

"Do what?" he asks. He is wearing the same jeans and black t-shirt he'd had on last night but now, somehow, they are miraculously clean.

"Just show up," I say. "Come into the kitchen like that, at the height of the dinner rush." I sound like a punishing mother, someone trying to teach someone a lesson.

"Because I knew you'd be here then."

I have to admit that makes some sense. I look at his application. He has left the space for his address blank.

"Where do you live?" I ask.

"And it's true," he says. "You need me."

I am not afraid anymore. Last night, when I finally got a hold of myself and told him, "Fine, go back to the prep kitchen and help," it felt like I was doing something that absolutely needed to be done. It felt like we both needed help. Now he tells me that when the restaurant closed, he had gone to an all-night Laundromat and convinced two drunk girls to let him throw his clothes in with theirs. While his jeans and shirt washed and dried, he sat in his boxers reading the newspaper. They had given him two beers. I can imagine the whole scene, him charming them with his good looks and serious stare, their wanting to help him.

I hire him for a two week probationary period. I don't know him, don't know who he is or who he's been so I try to watch him when I can. I can tell he has worked in a restaurant like mine before, can tell by the way he handles the equipment in the prep kitchen, by his movements and his focus, by the fact that he never asks anyone any questions. But there is so much to do when you own a restaurant and today I am all over the place—in my office planning menus, then working on the books, in the stock room taking inventory, then the walk-in cooler doing the orders and much of the time I don't know what he's doing. I don't forget about him but I'm not always sure where he is.

In the late afternoon, I find him on the line. He has made a shimmering pea mousse to serve under my house salmon. I am surprised but then I am angry. I ask him who he thinks he is. I ask him how he made the mousse and he won't tell me and that is how I discover he is a trained chef. I am a trained chef and never share the recipes I've invented with anyone. I know all about the relationship between privacy, thievery and pride. Still, I find the secrecy insulting until he gives me a bite and I am whisked away on the pleasure of peas.

After the two weeks, I let him keep the job because there were mashed potato cups filled with foie gras, the pineapple-jalapeno salsa and Serrano Ham panini, the roasted marrow toasts, a peach bombe, old customer raves, new customers—younger and so hip—forming a line outside at night, willing to wait however long it took to be seated. In my restaurant.

He is quiet, never late. I don't know where he lives. Or what he does when he is not at work and sometimes I forget about him but then when I realize that he is at the restaurant during every shift, even the ones I don't pay him for, I start thinking about him all the time. This is my restaurant, I am the boss, so I ask him questions, try to figure him out.

He answers everything too vaguely. I think he thinks his life is none of my business. Maybe he is right. He is a good worker, that's all I need to know. Or maybe he is shy. I am shy, I get that. Then one day, out of the blue, he says he thinks we should close between 4 and 6, that that would give the kitchen time to regroup, the staff a chance to have a meal together. He's already prepared it—lentil soup, spinach salad, grilled ham and manchego cheese with roasted tomatoes and pesto. The food is so good, comfort food but with an indefinable touch. He tells me to sit down, next to him at the table with the staff, and I do. We eat.

I start to like him, and then I discover I like having him there. Everyone else likes him, too. He does his job in the back kitchen but then when I'm not looking, he helps everyone else with their jobs. He shows the waiters a new, more sophisticated way of laying the napkins on the tables. He teaches the bartenders to make a drink with vodka, shaved ice and shards of fresh ginger; they start to offer it as a house specialty and we can't keep up with the demand. He asks me if we can serve our scallop appetizer on the ceramic spoons I only use for private tastings. He cooks the staff meal, the family meal, every night.

One night he sees me struggling over the books in the office and he tells me he can help. He was right from the start, I need help. I let him install a program in my aging computer that transforms my bookkeeping into something I actually like to do. He smiles. He works the day shift but is still here for the whole night shift and the hostesses tell me the customers love him. At night he greets them, sometimes walks them to their tables. I can't explain why I didn't know he was doing this, how he managed to do so many things without my knowing even though I knew he was there. I am not sure why I am letting it happen except that I am so much less tired than I ever was before he came. And business is booming.

Last night I found a stack of our linen napkins layered and folded into the shape of a pillow in the basement storage room. It was on top of an oversized garbage bag he was obviously using for a blanket. When I confronted him, he said I saved his life.

And when I wake up one morning some weeks after to the sound of the water running in my shower, I wonder what has happened to my own life. For the first time in ten years, I am sleeping in my bed. We drink our coffee there. He shampoos my hair, reads comic books out loud, makes love to me as if I am something precious, rare and fragile, something he must take care not to break, as if he knows me. After, he rubs his white teeth barely over my skin and I am afraid that he will bite me but he never does and because he never does, I relax. I know I should be at least a little frightened but I'm not.

When we are not at my apartment, we are both at my restaurant working.

All I know for sure about his past is that something he won't talk about happened and when he came to me, he was jobless. Homeless. But instead of wondering how on earth I'd let a stranger, practically a boy, infiltrate my small life, I fall headfirst into the supreme relief of not having to do everything myself in order to keep everything going. I fall into having someone to sleep with at night. Now I never look for him, wonder where he is. Like magic, he appears without warning beside me wherever I am—the line, the prep kitchen, the salad station—puts his arm around my waist and presses into me. Kisses me on the mouth. I do not know who I am. I think I am falling in love.

I discover he is a wizard with numbers so I let him oversee the purchasing. He is a whirlwind of energy and sometimes everywhere at once—the bar, the walk-in, the prep kitchen, the front of the house. I start to forget that he has not always been here, that we did not build this restaurant together. That I used to be alone.

Before he came, once in a while a guest would request to see the chef, and I'd tuck the wet sweaty hairs back into my headband, wipe my hands on my apron, and go out into the dining room to accept the compliments. But I had forgotten how to be social, comfortable only with people who worked for me and slipping in and out among the strangers in places I needed to go—the pharmacy, the grocery store, the dry cleaners. But he is so different, as easy and happy in his chef whites in the prep kitchen as he is in a suit in the dining room. Every restaurant needs someone like that.

He has even made some friends. A group of guys who eat dinner in the restaurant every Saturday night. He joins them. They are all unemployed chefs. I ask him if he thinks we should hire any of them but he says they are looking to start their own restaurant. At first, I like the stories he tells me about them. They are easy to listen to and I remember what it's like to have pals and I am happy for him. I never expected to be enough for him. But then one morning, over coffee before work, it hits me.

"Are these people you are going into business with?" I ask.

"Honey," he says, "I'm with you, aren't I?" He frowns, as if I am hurting him. "You're acting crazy."

Because I am crazy. I am living with someone fifteen years younger than I am, someone who appeared in my restaurant and knew exactly what was going to happen, assumed things I didn't know myself and was right. I went from working 15 hours a day without a break to spending an hour in the ocean every day at 3:00. I went from sleeping alone on my couch to spending nearly every waking and sleeping minute with a stranger who I thought was an illusion. I feel like he has always been here, that he is solid and I am safe. I didn't know I needed that kind of safety until it was there everyday.

I have a right to be crazy. I am middle-aged, bony. My face is thin, drawn. There are a lot of wrinkles. But this man touches it. He wipes it when it sweats, he moves the stray hairs from it, he looks right into it. He kisses it all the time.

"Maybe you are crazy," I say because when I think about this life, I know I don't understand. And then I don't want to think anymore so I say, "Maybe they are crazy. You don't really know these guys. They could be thieves."

I know an assortment of psychotics and thieves. They go anywhere they want with the extraordinary self confidence of the desperate who have nothing to lose or the stupidity to believe they will lose nothing. If they want money or liquor or sex, if they want to scare someone for real or just for kicks, if they merely want something to eat for free, they walk into places they don't belong and demand to be seen and to be served. In South Beach, where bums and drunks share the streets and beaches with celebrities and wealthy tourists, it is often hard to distinguish between the real threats and the mere expressions and that's what makes it so dangerous. Once I barred a mogul from entering my restaurant because he looked like a thug. Once I let a pair of thugs stay late in the bar because they looked like moguls; after we closed, they robbed two of my waitresses on the street. Some killers look only like thieves. Some thieves are a special kind of killer. I know these people, and I watch out for them.

So it makes me nervous to hear about these guys he eats dinner with every Saturday night, makes me wonder who they really are. I become afraid for him, start to think that he is being conned. I know he picks up the tab for their dinners. I don't care about the money. I tell him to be careful because I want to protect him. He says, "Don't worry. I think people are basically good. You gave me a chance, didn't you? And I know them better than you knew me."

This is true. He'd come from a mystery I still know nothing about to the places—my restaurant and my home—that I know best. And he knew I would take him, and then trust him. His instincts are good.

I don't have any friends. I tell myself it is by choice though, truly, I have morphed into this solitary person without realizing it. After my husband left, I didn't know how to turn myself back into someone who could trust anyone again. I threw myself into culinary school and then into work. I like the people who work for me and I am glad to have them near me but before he came, I thought I only needed myself. I thought I knew myself, which is why I didn't sense my own loneliness creeping up on me. I never saw it coming and then, abracadabra, it disappeared.

Just like a thief, while I wasn't looking, he took away all of the things I had been afraid of. And he replaced them with the things I had forgotten ever wanting, like coming home and having a brandy and listening to music with my aching feet in someone's lap instead of falling asleep on the couch in my chef clothes, having sworn off my bed years ago. Like having someone to walk home with after work, to scramble late night eggs for, someone to touch, who wanted to touch me. Slowly, subtly, bit by bit, he took me and left me fearless.

I think I am lucky, blessed. That somehow someone or something divine decided that I deserve this life I am living, really living, now. But then the spell is broken because the one morning, I wake up alone. I want it to be a dream. It isn't the first time I close my eyes to conjure back what I think I can't live without but before him, I had sworn it would be the last time. Back then, before the restaurant, before the work, when I learned that I was the kind of woman it was easy to leave, I had crumbled. Then I had begged and pleaded and promised to do anything to fix myself, to make myself right. Even though I did not know what was wrong.

This time, I am ready for a fight. By the time I get to the restaurant, my teeth are rattling. It is a steamy summer morning but I am shivering. I go back into the kitchen and he comes out from behind the line; it is clear he has been there for hours. He's reorganized the walk-in cooler and now everything we need is in clear view. He's dusted all the bottles in the bar. He's taken the crate of lemons that had begun to spoil and made forty individually-sized citrus cakes for the dinner service. It is seven in the morning and the rest of the staff won't be in until ten. In the dining room, he's set a table for two with a bottle of champagne chilling. He pulls lobster burritos from the oven and feeds me mine while he explains that sometimes when he can't sleep, he just needs to work. I understand this because it is true for me too but it doesn't take away the ache and panic. I am so angry. After the first bite, I say, "Feeding me is hokey," because I am so unsettled by the way I love it. But he is undaunted. He says, "You think this is hokey?" and leads me downstairs to the office where he has blown up an air mattress and lit candles.

The last time I had felt this way was the first time and I knew nothing. I was so young, thought it would last forever, didn't understand how love can be consumed by fear and instead of stomping it out like a fire, I stoked it, tended it, fed its restlessness bite by bite so that it could never be satisfied and never be finished. I was so frantic trying to keep the fire alive that I didn't see it growing out of control.

He says, "Look, I know I scared you. I'm sorry. But everyone comes to everyone with a history. We're learning how we are together, but we're still who we were before."

I don't know who he was before. And I had left who I was before a long time ago. I replaced her with someone who saved her heart for taste and texture and smell. Who used her head for everything else. Who made things make sense. Making sense is what saved me, sustained me. It's what pulled me out of the ashes and wed me to a career that relies on all the properties of fire. It's what recreated me into a person surrounded by people, by cooks and waiters and bartenders and dishwashers and vendors and customers, so I didn't know

I was alone. What I learned, in addition to how to cook, was that every time something went wrong, if I could make sense of it I could make it right. I didn't take chances until I let a stranger into my kitchen, into my bed.

I made sense of him. He was young but already too tired. He wanted stability. He wanted to make a life with someone in an industry he loved and understood. He knew how to operate every piece of equipment, how to increase profits, how to train cooks and servers. He was a fabulous, inspiring, inventive cook. He could butcher meat, he could skin a Dover sole in one move, he could suspend caviar in sabayon as easily as he could make grilled cheese. These things made him happy and they made sense to me. He knew that by just giving me a bite of something I hadn't had before, I would cave. That my heart would take over. He knew how to get there.

So when I get to the restaurant this morning, after having been with him for over a year and a half, and my key won't turn in the lock, I know I am dreaming. About banana pancakes. I was not surprised that he left me in the middle of the night because since the first time, it has become a ritual and one I celebrate like a teenager. This morning I showered and shaved, put on lotion, perfume. I hope he is making banana pancakes because that's what I have a taste for. Banana pancakes with pecans and caramel syrup. I will let him feed them to me, bite by sweet bite, because I always do. Because I am certifiably hokey in love.

I try the key again and again and then so hard it actually snaps off in the lock. I look like a thief, trying to break into my own restaurant. It is only seven in the morning and no one is out on the street yet. I cup my hands to either side of my face like blinders and peer inside. The lights are all out and so it gives the illusion that nothing is there, that my restaurant is an empty room. Like when I first started, when I had been emptied out and bought a space I could fill. The tables and chairs seem to have vanished. Maybe he moved them. Maybe he is redecorating the dining room or washing the carpet. I knock. And wait. I knock again, and call out his name. No one comes. So I knock again and again and again, each time harder and then harder than that so that he will hear me, emerge from wherever he is and make the fear starting to smoke and smolder inside me curl back into ash.

A police car cruises by and the officer gets out and asks to see some ID but I have nothing that says this space belongs to me. My key is broken in a lock where it didn't fit. My face is wet so I know I am crying and my teeth are clenched and they hurt—everything hurts—and then without seeing it coming, I start screaming, appear crazy, delusional, all the kinds of crazy I know, like someone to fear. Me. Someone to fear.

The cop pats my shoulder and asks me to calm down. When I do, he looks through the window and then asks me to tell him what is inside my restaurant. My description does not match what he sees.

"There's no stained glass hanging there, maam."

"What about the coffee station?" I say. "In the back corner? The espresso machine, regular coffee maker, two pots, one for decaf..." I rattle off my inventory like an auctioneer.

"Nothing back there, maam. Nothing at all. Is there someone we can call?"

Of course, there is! I think. *Call him. We've been robbed! He is probably tied up somewhere in the restaurant, waiting to be saved. Why didn't I think of this before? How much time have I wasted? He trusts everyone. He would have let anyone in. He could be dead in there!*

I recite his cell phone number and while the officer dials, I wipe my eyes and gather my strength and stand up straight. *I'm coming, don't worry. I'm here. I'm coming,* but a message on his cell phone says it's been disconnected. I paid the bill last week.

"Is there anyone else?" he asks me.

Anyone else? No, no one. There is no one else.

"Uh, ma'am?" he says, because I have not answered him and am staring into the black window, my place. "An employee maybe? A manager?"

Yes, there are employees. Waiters and dishwashers. There are hostesses, line cooks, two sous chefs, busboys, a sommelier on the weekends. There are day managers and night managers. Sometimes there is a harpist in the dining room, a quartet in the bar lounge. There are lots of people, really nice people, who come here every day and night to eat. An entire world of wonderful people.

I want to tell him this but don't know how when I look up and see Adele, the night manager, standing there. I hear her identifying herself, asking what's wrong. I hear her identifying me. I hear her saying she is here early because she left her cell phone in the hostess stand last night and needs it now to call her mother. I wonder why she didn't just call her mother from her home. I wonder what would have happened if we had been naked on the air mattress in my office, eating banana pancakes with our fingers, hearing someone upstairs rummaging around the hostess stand. We would have thought we were being robbed. *We have been robbed.*

Another policeman comes and together the two men bust open the door and Adele and I walk in. Adele says "oh my God oh my God" over and over again. I do not speak. Adele starts walking around the dining room, touching the walls, moving one hand over the other as if the missing tables, chairs, linens, vases, flatware will miraculously reappear from behind the dusky pink wallpaper I put up myself. In my lonely days. When I thought I was safe.

Poof. Everything has disappeared. There is nothing in the dining room, the bar, the lounge. All the plates and glassware, the water pitchers, the creamers and sugar bowls, the cream and sugar. Gone. The kitchen is an empty stainless steel vault. The huge Hobart to the tiny paring knives, the pots and pans, the tongs and spatulas and slotted spoons, and strainers, everything has vanished. The food is gone, the steaks and chops and fish and ribs, potatoes and onions and garlic, all the oils and vinegars, the spices and herbs, the truffles, pates, flour, butter, yeast, milks, the extracts. The walk-in cooler is cleaned out, except for a crate of rotting lemons.

I pull one out and my fingers fall through the soft blue and white mold to the decomposing flesh with its rancid sorry smell. How did he ever use these to make cakes? He was a magician. I sit down on the cooler floor, the terrible lemon in my palm, and try to turn magic into sense. Sleight of hand.

The police are asking me questions, but their words are jumbled and meaningless so I can't answer. They turn to Adele, who is crying. I hear her say his name, describe him, but the description doesn't sound like anyone I know.

The bigger of the two policemen very gently slides his hands under my arms and lifts me up. He walks me into the dining room, forgetting there is nowhere to sit, and just as gently settles me onto the carpet that apparently could not be pried up in time.

"Is there anything I can get you?"

But what can you pull out of thin air?

"Can we call someone else?" the officer asks. I try to conjure up the image of his Saturday night friends, men I never met. He could not have done this alone. I hear Adele rattling off names and numbers.

"Ok. Good," I hear the officer say. "We'll call them. In the meantime, do you want to go get your boss something? A cup of coffee? She needs something."

What do you need when everything is gone?

Something small. Just one small thing, something that I could make disappear, something irreplaceable that would be gone for good. The tip of a finger. The bottom pearl of an ear. A toe, something I could run my teeth across and then bite off, clean and fast. A real thing, a real loss, that by being gone would say over and over again, forever, that I had been there.

CandyLand

Candace is an executive vice president at a private bank. She is a person of position. A woman with power. She is 60 years old. Her clients are the wealthiest people in Miami: they are, the women and the men, thin and elegant. Their grooming is flawless. Even the elderly ones, some with wrinkles the surgery just could not take away, are more beautiful than any beautiful ordinary person could be. They are self-important, entitled, often rude. They can be judgmental. Mean. Candace is often amazed at how ugly they are inside. But she knows exactly how to handle them, how to soothe them, coo and compliment them into her fold. She has infinite patience. No matter what they say or how they say it, Candace is always kind. She is very good at her job.

Candace has a team of young associates who do all the real research and investing. Candace has taught them everything she knows. What she does not know is that behind her back, they call her Candy Ass. She does not know that they do not believe she has a husband named Edward who lives abroad. She does not know that they find her too loud, too inappropriate, that they inhale through their mouths when she is talking to them because they think she has bad breath. She does not know that they cringe when they see her coming, that they dread her stories about her tiny dogs and their funny ways, her crazy old aunts in the Midwest, her romance with Edward. She does not see how hard it is for them to smile at the coy innuendo, the batted eyelashes, the large hand attached to the large wrist with all the bangles fanning the air near her neck to signal the temperature of her and Edward's reunions.

She has invited all of them to her St. Patrick's Day Party. She invited her boss Mr. Kramer and his wife, too. She invited all of the people on her floor at the bank. She designed the invitation on the Internet and sent it by email: it featured a leprechaun frozen in mid-jig and said ATTENDANCE AND FUN REQUIRED!!

The little dogs, Fred and Wilma, trot around her feet as she works in the kitchen. Each one is wearing a bright green sweater. The white potatoes are peeled and in ice water; she will begin to cook them at 5:00, an hour before the party starts. The corned beef and cabbage looks delicious but it is making the house smell. Candace isn't worried; she'll spray the rooms with perfume before her guests arrive. The Irish Soda Bread is baked and sliced and in foil so Candace can pop it in the oven just before serving. The veggies and dip, cheese cubes and shrimp trays from Publix are in the fridge; the green iced cookies are already on the table. Candace has bought potato chips, pretzels, peanuts and pork rinds and placed them in bowls all over her house. She needs to take a shower and get dressed but first she decides she'll make the salad.

She chops iceberg lettuce, scallions, cucumbers and green peppers, an entirely green salad. She's bought Green Goddess dressing, a nice St. Paddy's Day touch. The bar is set up, the keg with the green beer will be delivered around 4:00. At 3:30, she goes upstairs to shower and dress. She had thought about dressing as a leprechaun but then decided on a green jumpsuit with a gold lame belt, sparkly gold sandals, and green and gold dangling shamrock earrings. More hostess-appropriate. Candace likes to do things right.

She is a very large woman. Her mother and father had named her Candy, a confection. But she was not the daughter her mother envisioned. As a child, and then a teenager, Candy wanted to please her mother, who told her endlessly that no one took fat people seriously, that she needed to watch her figure. Powerless, she watched it grow and grow. Candy wanted to make her mother proud but she couldn't because her parents were too much in love. They were so much in love that there wasn't enough room for their child, especially such a big child. The parents had been thin and elegant like Candace's clients but they were much poorer and despite their nightly walks and careful eating, they both had small bad hearts. Candy knew how hard it was to take care of the heart and vowed to keep hers big and good. When her parents died, in a car accident on the way home from visiting her aunts in Omaha, Candy was 23. Then she disappeared inside Candace, whose imagination always precedes her.

While Candace showers, she imagines the look on everyone's faces when they walk into her party. She has set up the rented tables with green cloths and gold Chiavari chairs in the living room. Each table has a St. Patrick's center-piece and a glittery gold and green leprechaun hat for every guest. She has enough food to feed an army, or at least an entire floor of a bank.

Candace loves her job. She is always having to figure out ways to help the bank be better, to please her difficult and sometimes irrationally unreasonable clients, but her best and brightest idea as far as she is concerned was training her staff of six to do what she did for most of her career there: that she considers a gift she gave to the institution that took her in as a brand new MBA and nurtured her rise to management.

But banks are suffering all across the country and Candace's is no different. Mr. Kramer had told her he was considering laying some people off in the near future. "Not any of my people," she had said firmly and he had responded, "we'll have to see." But there was nothing to see. Candace was devoted to her staff and she knew how to take care of them. They were family and she would make sure their jobs were safe, even if it meant upsetting Mr. Kramer. Stan Kramer. He was her age and hired only a few months before she started at the bank, over thirty years ago, but because he was her boss, she always called him Mr. Kramer. All these years.

He had asked to see her yesterday. Candace assumed it was because his wife was wondering what they should bring to the party.

"Nothing at all but an appetite," she had said, as she walked into his office.

"Pardon?" he said.

"Oh," she said.

"Candace," he began, "I need to discuss something serious with you."

"All right," she said, and sat down across from him, pulling her flowing gauze skirt down over her knees.

"But first," she said, "you and Mrs. K will be coming to my party tomorrow night, won't you? You didn't RSVP so I wanted to make sure." The truth is no one had RSVPd: her staff told her daily they were planning to come but still had a few things to work out and might have to stop at another party first, and all the other people at the bank whom she invited waved to her when she walked by their desks or offices and gave her the thumbs up sign. If she saw them in the hallways or the cafeteria, they all asked how the plans for the party were coming so Candace assumed they were all in. Young people didn't appreciate the courtesies her generation lived by, like responding to an invitation.

"Oh, your party, your St. Patrick's Day Party," Mr. Kramer said, "Yes, of course, we . . . we will definitely be stopping by."

"Come hungry," Candace said, "there's going to be tons of food."

Mr. Kramer shifted uncomfortably in his chair. "Good, sounds good."

"So what did you want to see me about?"

Mr. Kramer looked down at the papers on his desk. Candace was prepared to stand firm against his even suggesting that she fire any of her staff. Her department had more accounts than any of the other bank executives, accounts she had cultivated and nurtured, and she needed everyone on her team to keep all of her clients happy. Over the years, her department had evolved into such a well-oiled machine that their jobs were almost interchangeable. Her staff managed all the accounts and Candace oversaw them but focused on the personal nature of those client relationships, and on the more difficult situations. Sure, she could return to the work her team was doing if she had to lose anyone, but she would fight that tooth and nail—not because she was lazy but because she was proud of her team and of her desire to fight for each and every one of them to the bitter end. She was exactly the kind of boss she wanted to be, the kind of person she admired—someone who is loyal, trustworthy, who people can depend upon. A good person with a big heart.

"There's no easy way to say this, Candace," Mr. Kramer began, "but the bank is having some financial difficulties now and . . ."

"Mr. Kramer," Candace interrupted, inching forward on her chair and sitting up so straight that her entire torso was a fortress. She knew how to use her power, how to be taken seriously. "I understand. But I have to tell you, before you even suggest it, that I cannot operate without my staff. My entire team. Together, they take excellent care of our clients. Each one has a talent and a purpose that we, the bank, simply cannot do without. It's not possible for me to let any of them go." She was pleased with herself, the firm voice that settled even the most entitled clients, the way she stuck up for her staff and made it clear she would not bend. She leaned back then and smiled.

"I know that," he said. He shuffled the papers around, then set them down and looked Candace directly in the eye. "This is not about your team."

Candace sits in the living room waiting for the green beer delivery. She is dressed and likes the way her shamrock earrings tinkle when she moves her head from side to side. The room looks bright and festive. She is so pleased. She tries to remember the last time she was this excited.

It was the night she graduated from MBA school, over thirty years ago, when she thought Ray was going to propose. She was twenty-eight then and Ray, who had been her father's mechanic, had been living with her in the house for five years. They had met right after Candace's parents died. He thought it was his fault because he had tuned up their car right before they left for Omaha and maybe something went wrong. He said he was really sorry. He didn't know what else to say. He refused to let Candace pay her father's bill. Candace invited him to dinner.

From the minute he walked in, Candace liked having him there. He was a big man who liked Candace's cooking. He lived in a small room above the garage where he worked but he looked at home in her little house. Candace felt at home, too, watching him smoking a cigarette after the meal, his bare feet on the coffee table.

After the graduation ceremony, Candace had scanned the sea of students, parents, relatives, friends and faculty at the reception on the lawn for Ray but she couldn't find him anywhere. Finally, she saw him leaning against their car in the parking lot, smoking a cigarette. As she made her way across the lawn, unsteady in the high skinny heels she had bought for the occasion, Ray looked up and waved. She waved back. She'd had a manicure the day before, to show off the ring.

She asked him how he liked the ceremony and he said, "What?" and then, "Oh, yeah, ok. Just fine. Liked it fine. You did real good." Then he told her she should take the hat off because sweat was falling down on her face from underneath it.

She said, "Mortar board" then was sorry because Ray hated it when she tried to teach him things. It was June in Miami, hot and humid. There was no breeze. She took the mortar board off and said, "Let's get home. I have champagne!"

When they got home, she changed out of her graduation robe and put on a magenta silk matching pajama and robe set and followed her imagination downstairs. Ray was already on the couch, smoking and watching wrestling. Candace pulled the bottle of Veuve Cliquot out of the refrigerator and set it down on the coffee table with two crystal flutes she'd purchased at Bloomingdale's, ones she had decided upon for her bridal registry. She poured the champagne and said, "here's to us" hoping that would be a cue for Ray to produce the engagement ring that glittered in her head. Ray swung his feet off the coffee table—presumably to join her in the toast—knocking his glass to the floor. The Veuve soaked into the carpet.

"Never mind," he said. "I'll get a beer."

Ray was sloppy. Most of the time, he didn't shave. Candace liked his arms, how she could see the muscles and veins in them. Ray liked fat women, like to grab their asses during sex. Candace liked the way Ray looked in his gas station uniform. She was about to take a job at the Turnberry Bank and she liked how Ray thought it was fine if she made more money than he did, his relief that the house had long been paid for, that he came home for dinner every night even if he went out again right after.

When Ray returned with his beer, he said, "yeah, here's to us" but when he opened the beer, it sprayed all over Candace's new lingerie, causing dark splotches to form in the silk. He said, "Sorry, girl but, hey, it don't matter. Now you'll make some real money and you can buy more of them things."

The doorbell rings at 4:00. The guys delivering the keg say, "Whoa, you're in the spirit" when they see Candace's outfit and all the decorations. She says "Top o' the mornin' to ya boys" and giggles. She follows them to the deck where they will set up the keg. Before they leave, she will offer them a green beer.

When Ray left Candace for a waitress named Rae, a plain heavy girl who used to serve them wings at the bar they went to on Friday nights, Candace waited months for him to come home because she was sure he would. She worked all day at the bank and that was fine but at night and on the weekends, she didn't know what to do with herself. Not that Ray was home that much at night or on the weekends but he was there all the same.

To make the time pass, she cooked and froze all his favorite foods—stew, enchiladas, chili—and bought a freezer for the garage dedicated to them. She read romance novels, did crossword puzzles, had a deck built on the back porch that she planned to turn into a smoking lounge for him. She washed their car every weekend, and organized her cupboards and closets weekly, giving everything she knew she didn't need to the poor. When the small house began to look too empty, she started to collect ceramic figurines and hired her neighbor's son to build shelves for them. When months went by, she bought the two small dogs and dressed them in small dog outfits. When years went by, she bought herself an engagement ring, invented Edward, and fed her dogs defrosted portions of the food she'd cooked for Ray.

"Won't this be fun, Mr. & Mrs. Flintstone?" Candace says to the dogs while she sips a green beer. Fred and Wilma seem very excited, too. Some thirty guests have been invited and Candace has cooked for at least fifty, so everyone can take some leftover food home.

Candace wishes her parents were still alive for tonight. They never wanted to throw parties, to spend the money, to have people in their home. They were always afraid of too much food. But if they were here tonight, they would see how Candace has transformed the house into an Irish wonderland. They would meet all the people from the bank and see what she has made of her life. They would not be able to help but be proud. She is glad that Ray will not be here. He would just embarrass her. Edward has so much more class.

At 5:00 she puts the potatoes on simmer, pops the bread into a warm oven and pours herself another green beer. Then she sits in her living room, admires the green streamers and shamrocks, and waits. The dogs sit at her feet, panting.

It isn't a question of money. She has no mortgage, no car payments, no credit card debt. Over all the years of waiting and working and saving and investing, she's accumulated more money than she could ever spend in what's left of her lifetime and the retirement package the bank has offered her is beyond generous. And it isn't that she doesn't understand the Board's thinking:

she fully comprehends costs and benefits and the concept of early retirement, how her doing that makes more fiscal sense than getting rid of any member of her team because in addition to managing the clients, each one does two or three other essential jobs as well.

"It's not personal, Candace," Mr. Kramer had said, "everyone here thinks very highly of you and you've done a wonderful job for us. It's business, financial. Plus, you deserve this, time to yourself to do . . . the things you love to do."

She had listened quietly and sat very still while he spoke. She was not at all upset. She was having a party the next day and after that, she would figure out what to do. She was a valued member of the bank; they wouldn't be where they were if it hadn't been for her.

Mr. Kramer was still talking, saying something about early retirement, when she said, "Thirty-two years."

"Thirty-two excellent years," Mr. Kramer agreed. Then he stood to shake her hand.

Candace had gone into her office and dusted all of her things—her coffee mugs, little porcelain dogs, snow globes, books, plants, the framed photos of her with various clients that covered an entire wall. She did an inventory of the snacks in her snack drawer. She ate a package of beef jerky. Then she sat at her desk and looked out the window on downtown Miami. She tried to remember the last time she had been to the beach. That was not one of the things that she loved to do. What she loved to do was work at the bank. She had never thought Stan Kramer was all that clever and she had always known that it was her effectiveness that made him seem successful but she was too good to ever say so.

She had stopped by everyone's desk, calling out brightly, "See you tomorrow, 6:00 sharp!" interpreting the startled look on her colleagues' faces as surprise that she was leaving so early. The workday might be over at 5:00, but Candace never left the office before 7:00.

"Hey, I know it's only 5:00 but if I don't get home and start cooking, you won't have anything to eat at the party!"

It is 7:15 before the doorbell rings but Candace hasn't noticed because she has been drinking the green beer, humming along to the Irish music on the stereo, rearranging her family photos and the ones she has come up with for

Edward, who is trying as hard as he can to leave Switzerland in time to get to the party. When she goes to the door, Mr. and Mrs. Kramer are standing on her front steps; Mrs. Kramer has a bottle of wine tied with a green bow. The dogs are trying to jump up on her and she is lifting her feet, one after the other, to try and dissuade them.

"Oh, you bad dogs," Candace says, "let Mrs. Kramer come in."

"You look so . . . festive," Mrs. Kramer says.

"Sorry we're so late," Mr. Kramer says, "but our son had a little St. Paddy's Day dinner so we stopped by there to see our grandkids first. Hope it's ok."

"Of course, it's ok, come in," Candace says and hearing the word dinner, remembers her potatoes that have been simmering on the stove for two hours.

"Mashed potatoes then, even better," Candace says, and walks into the kitchen, leaving her guests alone in the living room.

"Are we the first ones here?" Mr. Kramer asks, hesitantly. He is thinking that at least her own staff would have stopped by. He felt it was the least they could do.

When Candace hears his question, the full weight of what is happening begins to descend and the steam from the pot of potatoes rises up and into her face. The heat makes her angry. *Look around, fool* she thinks but says, "Yes you are!" She pours the potatoes into a colander and then puts them back into the hot pot. She adds milk and butter, salt and pepper, and begins to mash them. She is mashing them so hard that lumps of hot potato and spatters of milk fly out of the pot, landing on her green jumpsuit.

"Hope you're hungry," she calls out, and it sounds almost like she's singing.

Mr. and Mrs. Kramer are still standing in the living room. They have not taken their coats off and Mrs. Kramer is still holding the wine.

"There's beer on the deck," Candace says.

"Oh, ok, thanks," Mr. Kramer says. He motions to his wife and they take off their coats, set them on the couch, and head toward the deck. They pass Candace in the kitchen, pulling the veggie and cheese and shrimp trays out of the refrigerator. As she puts them on the table, she calls out, "I'll have another beer, too, while you're in there."

The Kramers come and stand beside her at the buffet table and Mr. Kramer gives her a beer. Candace says, "thank you" and "help yourself to appetizers while I get dinner together" and Mrs. Kramer is about to say, "we just ate at our son's" but she thinks better of it and picks up a shrimp.

"Have more beer," Candace says, as if the Kramers have been there for hours. "I'll be right out." She brings out the platter of corned beef and cabbage, the bowl of mashed potatoes with three more pats of butter melting in its center, the salad tossed in too much Green Goddess dressing, and a basket of the Irish Soda Bread. The buffet's fullness pleases her.

"Oh, wait a minute," Candace says, and she goes back into the living room; when she returns, she is carrying two St. Patrick's Day plastic hats.

"Put these on," she says to the Kramers, in a voice that has become too bright. Mr. Kramer laughs a little and Mrs. Kramer puts one of her hands up to her styled hair.

"Put them on," Candace says, and now that voice has turned military. This is a new level of seriousness for Candace. She has never used this voice before because she has never had to.

The Kramers take the hats and put them on.

"Well, then," Candace says, "Let's eat." She fills three plates with heaping piles of the food she's made.

"Here you go," she says, handing them each a plate. Then Candace pulls three of the Chiavari chairs from the living room up to the buffet and motions for the Kramers to sit down.

"Why don't we take our plates to the living room?" Mr. Kramer asks. "The tables look so nice in there."

"Look at all this food," Candace says, thinking that Stan Kramer is more stupid than she has thought he was all these years. "There's enough for fifty people. How are we going to eat all this food? Well, if we just sit right here at the buffet, we won't have to get up to get more. We can just dig right in."

Candace digs in.

"This is so good," she says, as if she were a guest.

"Yes, it is," Mrs. Kramer says, while she and her husband move their forks around the mounds on their plates, lifting small bites to their mouths periodically; they have just eaten and only stopped by because Mr. Kramer felt so guilty about firing Candace. Even though he had told everyone at the bank that Candace would not be returning, he had asked them to at least show up to her party. That they had not is making his already high blood pressure rise. He looks down at his plate, at the kind of food he and his wife never eat. In addition to high blood pressure, Mr. Kramer has high cholesterol and Mrs. Kramer is forever watching her weight.

Candace looks at them, her mouth full of corned beef.

"Not quite what you expected, eh?" she says.

"It's all delicious," Mr. Kramer says, "but you know . . ."

"The others will be here soon," Candace says, "I think they all had to stop somewhere else first. Just like you. St. Patrick's Day is like Thanksgiving, a big family holiday. I'm going to make my party a tradition. I didn't know it before but it's really something I love to do. I just hope when everyone gets here they're hungry. And if his plane is on time, Edward will be here soon . . . you must wait and meet him. Eat up!"

Mrs. Kramer can no longer contain herself. "Actually, Candace, you know, we just ate at our son's and . . ."

"You will love Edward," Candace says, thinking it is rude to eat at someone else's house when you are going to a party. I would never do something like that, Candace thinks to herself. "Everyone loves Edward. And he cannot wait to meet you. All of you. Though this is even too much food for our whole bank to eat tonight, I don't know what I was thinking. Not to worry, though, I can bring the leftovers into work on Monday."

Candace is rambling because there is a disconnect between what she is thinking and what she is saying. And because she is taking bites and breaths as she goes along.

"As long as Edward doesn't scarf them all up in the middle of the night. He's a middle of the night eater, that one," and she laughs the way women do when their lovers have bad habits they find endearing. "But so skinny . . . well, not skinny, more slim, a fine build. He takes such good care of himself."

When the Kramers don't respond, she continues. "And the dogs," she says, pointing at the poodles who are sitting at her feet. "Not to worry, though: look how small they are. I'll just give them a few potatoes," and with her fingers, she takes two clumps of mashed potatoes and tosses them on the carpet. "But this food is best when you eat it right now, while it's fresh and hot," she adds, leaning over to pile more meat and potatoes onto her plate. "You know, I was going to make boiled potatoes, that's traditional with corned beef and cabbage, but I think mashed are better, don't you?"

The Kramers sit dumbfounded on the rented chairs, full plates of heavy food clotting on their laps.

"Don't you?" Candace repeats, as if they didn't hear her the first time.

"Mashed are, yes, they're better. Definitely," Mr. Kramer is looking at his wife now who is mouthing the words, *let's go.*

"But they don't keep well," Candace continues, "but, you know what? If there's any leftover, if you two don't eat them all, I'll make patties out of them and fry them up at the bank for lunch on Monday."

"About Monday," Mr. Kramer says, setting his full plate down on the buffet.

Candace stands up, picks up Mr. Kramer's plate, and returns it to him.

"Eat." Candace has never been commanding. It was never her style. Her style was nurturing, not punishing. But there was so much real pleasure in this that she was sorry that she hadn't discovered it a long time ago.

"You, too," she says to Mrs. Kramer, whose first name is Grace. "You're too skinny as it is."

"Well, I . . ." Mrs, Kramer stammers.

"You know, Grace, it's so nice to see you," Candace says. Her words are clipped, snarling almost, satisfying. It is a relief to finally feel this way.

"I never get to see you, Grace. I always thought we would be friends, you and I. I can't believe over all these years, thirty-two years, we've never spent any time together." She sits down again and dips a large piece of soda bread from her plate into the butter stick on the buffet table and stuffs it in her mouth. "You've never invited me over to your house. Why is that, Grace? Why do you think we never became friends?"

Mrs. Kramer quickly puts of forkful of soggy salad into her mouth. She raises her shoulders a little, goes down for another forkful of something else.

"I have an idea," Candace says, happy that she is having such a good time at her own party, that in the end it was worth all of the work. "Why don't you come down to the bank next week and we'll go out to lunch."

Mrs. Kramer nods her head and sticks her fork into the pile of corned beef on her plate. She looks as though she is going to throw up.

Mr. Kramer looks up at Candace. The look on her face frightens him. "I think that's a fine idea," he says but it comes out in a whisper that can barely be heard.

"Pardon?" Candace says. If her parents were here tonight, they would see just how seriously she is taken.

"I said I think that's a fine idea," Mr. Kramer repeats.

If her parents were here, they would be beyond proud.

Dancing

Lucy heard Al's RV on the gravel of Hank's driveway Thursday at 3:00 in the morning but she didn't know what it was. When she opened her eyes, she saw Hank already had his jeans on and was pulling his pistol out of the bed stand drawer.

"Surprise Hankers," a woman was saying. There was banging on the front door. "Rise and shine!" Lucy stood behind Hank while he looked through the door's window. "For God's sake," he said, and opened the door.

"I could have killed you all," Hank said. "It would have been self-defense."

"Now where's the fun in that, honey?" the woman asked. She gave Hank a kiss on the cheek and came into the house.

"Home sweet old home," a man said, following her in. He looked old and frail and was walking on a cane.

"What up, Wanker?" This was a young guy, in his thirties, handsome and solid. Lucy had no idea what was going on.

"You could have called," Hank said to the man with the cane.

"You could have called," the younger guy said. "Saved us all this trouble."

"Oh honey," the woman said, "where are my manners?" She walked up to Lucy and took her hand. "I'm Big Mae, Hank's sister-in-law. This here's my husband Al, Hank's brother, and our son, Junior."

"So nice to meet you," Lucy said. She remembered Al Carlson from high school. He was two years ahead of her and they had never met but she and all her girlfriends had huge crushes on him because he was the captain of the football team. How frail he was now, so much smaller and thinner than the handsome athlete she remembered. How does the body disappear like that?

"Pleased to meet you, too," Al said. Then he slapped Hank on the shoulder and limped into the living room.

"Where's Maybelle?" Hank asked.

"Couldn't get off work," Big Mae said quickly.

"She works for you," Hank said.

"Believe what you want," Junior said.

"What are you doing here, anyway?" Hank asked.

"The time's come," Big Mae said, "to see you. Waterville."

"Which you'd of known if you ever called back," Junior said.

"I see you two dressed up for the occasion," Hank said, rolling his eyes at Al and Junior in their overalls and wife-beater t-shirts. "You drive up here in the middle of the night from Miami but you look like you just got off the train from Petticoat Junction."

"Keepin it real," Al said, and Junior chimed in, "you tell him, Pops."

"You're like the Unibomber here, bro," Al said, setting himself into the big leather lounge chair Lucy had surprised Hank with after their first month of dating. "Living out here. What're you cookin' up there on that computer of yours? Plans to blow up Waterville?" Once in the chair, Al pulled a long-necked Budweiser out of his overall bib, twisted off the top and took a big swig.

"Maybe you should knock off the beer, Al," Hank said. Al's arms were thin and bluish-white.

"A little late for that, I think," Al said, and took a long swig.

"How long are you staying?" Hank asked. Lucy thought he was being rude, though she wasn't surprised. Hank valued his privacy above almost anything else.

"Don't know yet. But tonight, we're going dancing at Sandalini's," Al announced.

"It's almost 4:00 in the morning," Hank said. Although no one had remarked about it, Hank still had the gun in his hand. He walked into the kitchen and stuck it in one of the drawers.

"Later, tonight. Dinner, dancing. I always like some good fun on a Friday night at Sandalini's."

Lucy loved Sandalini's and hoped they would invite her. In the middle of downtown Waterville, it was the closest thing to fun in a twenty mile radius. Before she started seeing Hank, Lucy went there on Fridays after work with her teacher friends for the oversized cocktails and deep-fried shrimp. The place was big and old school Italian, with red walls that had thick redder and raised designs in fake velvet, plastic flowers on the table, low lighting, peanuts on the bar, and a disco ball above the small dance floor. On Fridays, there was a local band that played oldies. Everyone thought the owner, Antonio Sandalini, was in the mafia.

Lucy discovered that Hank hated Sandalini's after their first date. He took her there because it was the only place in Waterville that wasn't a diner or a fast food joint. Lucy could see that Hank was angry and itchy the minute they stepped inside. She'd tried to make small talk during dinner but Hank only responded with short clipped answers and she wondered what she was doing that was making him so mad. When she ordered the cheesecake for dessert and asked if he'd like to share, he told her didn't eat dessert. She pushed it away and asked if he wanted to dance.

"I don't dance," Hank had said.

She thought she'd never see him again and she wasn't exactly sorry but the next week he called and asked if she wanted to come over and make dinner. She thought about saying no, ended up saying sure and over spaghetti and her homemade meatballs, Hank told Lucy why he hated Sandalini's.

"Stupid, backward, hillbilly," he'd said. "Just like this whole damn town." This was the town where Hank had been born and that tried to raise him but he got out as soon as he could. Later, she learned why he'd come back. Lucy understood him. He thought Sandalini's was beneath him. At the end of the night, he said he liked her, that she was a good cook, that maybe they could do this again the next Saturday night. That was nearly a year ago.

"I'm not giving that gangster any of my money," Hank said to Al but Al just shook his head and laughed. The overalls and bad English were a cover: Lucy knew Hank's brother Al was a millionaire. She also knew Hank didn't think it was fair.

"My treat," Al said.

"Have a blast," Hank said. "You need anything now? We're going back to bed."

"We'll find whatever we need," Big Mae said. "You go on back to sleep, honey. You too, Lucy. We'll get to know each other in the morning. I'll have some coffee for you. Sweet dreams."

"Dream about your dancing shoes, little brother," Al said.

❖

When Hank and Lucy came out of his bedroom at nine on Friday morning, Al and Big Mae and Junior were sitting at the kitchen island having coffee and cinnamon buns that Big Mae had made after they'd gone to sleep. She'd brought all the ingredients.

"Here's your java," Big Mae said, getting up and going to pour each of them a cup of coffee. "Come join us, you two. These buns are still warm."

"Warm your buns on these fancy stools," Al said. "What do you got all these stools for anyway? Planning on starting a family?"

Hank leaned against the island. Lucy stood behind him. She was nervous. She knew Hank had special ordered the stools from a Danish company he'd found on the Internet. They never sat on them.

"Have a cinnamon bun, honey," Big Mae said to Lucy. Hank took one and bit in.

"Good, Big Mae," he said.

"Just like your mamma's. You could never resist your mamma's baking."

Lucy wanted a cinnamon bun, too, but she refrained. Hank discouraged her from eating sweets because they were so fattening.

"What do you want to do today?" Al asked.

"I've got work to do," Hank said, though it wasn't true. Hank wasn't working. He was living off his credit cards and biding his time; he'd come back to Waterville from Colorado over a year ago, just before his mother died, because she'd left him the house in her will. He'd contacted a lawyer to find out how to get around the will's stipulation that he never sell the house and once he did, he'd pocket the money and move back to Aspen. He talked about it all the time.

"Then we'll stay here with you, pal," Al answered. "That's why we're here. We'll hang out and then get dolled up and go to Sandalini's."

"Why do you want to go there?" Hank said. "I hate that guy, I hate that place. You want to be here so let's stay here."

"You dance, Miss Lucy?" Al asked.

"Yes, I love it," Lucy said. She hadn't been dancing once since she started seeing Hank. Nearly everyone from their high school still lived in town and went dancing at Sandalini's all the time. Since she'd been attached to Hank, she knew he'd be angry if she ever went there. But if she went there with Hank and his family . . .

"No," Hank said. "We're not going there, Al. That's it."

Big Mae sighed. "Your brother likes the dancing, Hankers."

"You can dance here," he said. "I'll hum you a tune."

Al slapped Hank on the back and shook his head.

"Come on, honey," Big Mae said, "We really want you guys to come with us."

"Nothing doing, Big Mae. You all go. Lucy'll come over tomorrow and we can all have dinner here together then. How long did you say you were staying?"

"Until we're ready to go," Al said. "Get ready to jitterbug, buddy."

"Cinnamon buns are great, Mae. I've got to get to work now," Hank said.

"What kind of work you doing now, Wanker?" Junior asked. "Something for Money-in-the Bankers?"

"Enough with the nicknames, Junior," Hank said. "Think we've both out-grown that now."

"Naw, not me. Haven't seen you in like, what? Ten years? But you'll always be Hankers, Wanker, Money-in-the-Bankers to me."

"He thought he was clever when he was a kid," Hank said to Lucy, who could not imagine anyone getting away with calling Hank anything other than Hank.

"Still clever now," Junior said.

"Yeah, that's why you're still living with your parents, right?" Hank said, and when he did, Lucy could practically see all the joking around disappear into black.

"*Back* with my parents," Junior said. "With my mother. And my father. Your brother. Get it?"

"I have work to do," Hank said. He was already in the hall near his office. Over his shoulder, he said, "Lucy?"

"Home to feed my cat. See you all tomorrow."

Lucy knew Hank didn't love her. He didn't even really seem to like much about her except that she was there. It was obvious to her that Al was dying. Probably cancer. Hank often thought he had cancer. Or that he was having a heart attack. Or a stroke. Sometimes he said his vision went blurry. Often he had pains in his chest, sometimes in his arms and legs. Sometimes he had trouble breathing. During the week, Lucy would call him every morning at eight and again every evening at five to see how he was doing. Her checking in calmed him down. On Saturdays, she brought over groceries, cooked dinner, and spent the night. It was their routine. Though sometimes he called her in a panic in the middle of the night.

At first, she could not figure out why he had picked her. She was so surprised when he asked her out to dinner that day at that grocery store that she just said yes, immediately, before her alarms went off. His good looks made Lucy uncomfortable. And while Lucy had been adorable in high school, a place where she shined and didn't have time for the bad boy Hank Carlson, what life ended up giving her had made her chubby and puffy. She had that roll of skin around her neck, flabby arms and what the younger teachers called 'muffin tops,' the extra weight on what was left of her waistline. She tried to take care of herself, bought the designer clothes at Value City, had her hair and nails and toes done once a week in downtown Waterville. And it all seemed fine until she started seeing Hank. Hank was too handsome for someone like her. She knew he thought so, too. It was ironic, all the years of trying to look good for some chance encounter and then when it comes, the effort just feels embarrassing.

Hank was always telling Lucy that he was getting ready to go. To pack up, move back to Colorado. He'd be taking his Danish barstools but not her. He made that very clear though he needn't have bothered. Lucy was not stupid. She knew he didn't want to be in Waterville and she knew she was about as far from his type as she could be. Hank's persistent efforts to improve her—his "suggestions" about her weight and her hair, his fawning over actresses on TV—were hurtful, but by the time he was comfortable enough to say those things to her, they were in the routine which broke up her own lonely life in a way she discovered she needed. Waterville was a small town that people moved out of but hardly anyone moved into. In a few years, she would be fifty. She liked being the person Hank depended on. She liked cooking for him, cleaning up, settling in on the couch with her magazines while he watched TV. She liked these nights in a nice old house with a man who didn't kiss her but who, when she woke up in the mornings, had been holding on to her in his sleep.

❖

When Lucy got home, the phone was ringing.

"Are you all right?" she asked Hank.

"Yeah, sure," he said.

"Your family is so nice. I'm really happy for you that they're here."

"Easy on the enthusiasm," he said. "So dinner tomorrow, all right?"

"Yes, I can't wait," Lucy said, even though she knew it wasn't what he wanted to hear. But she was excited to have the chance to throw a party. When she was young, she was really good at it. "Do you want me to make anything in particular?"

"Yeah, steak. They're big eaters. And you should probably bring a dessert."

"Great. I'll bake a cake. So what are you going to do tonight?" She knew they would never be able to talk Hank into going to Sandalinis.

"We're going to . . . get a pizza."

"Oh, ok then," Lucy said. She wanted him to invite her. They normally didn't spend Friday nights together but the night before Hank had called her just before midnight because he had chest pains so she had come right over. By the time she got there, he was fine so they watched some TV and went to bed. She was there when his family arrived. She knew them now. So why not just invite her over tonight, too?

"Look, honey, my brother Al . . . he's, uh, he's sick."

"Yes, I know. I could tell. He really doesn't look well."

"Yeah, he's pretty sick. You know . . ." The words *my brother has cancer* were lodged in his head but they would not travel the distance.

"Sure, I know." Lucy was quiet for a second and touched. She didn't think Hank had it in him but now she could see he wanted some time just with his family. "I totally understand. I'm so sorry."

"Not your fault," Hank said.

Lucy had been a party girl when she was young. She liked to have fun. She often marveled with her friends about how even as they aged, they all still felt the same way they did when they were in their twenties. No matter what anyone says, that's the hardest thing about getting old. Not feeling old. Not believing it. Looking into the mirror and wondering who was looking back.

After hanging up with Hank, Lucy thought about calling Nan and Nicole and seeing if they wanted to do happy hour at Sandalinis. It would be fun to go, it had been so long, and she could get to know Big Mae and Al and Junior a little better. But then she thought better of it, knew how angry Hank would be—he would think it was a betrayal. So, instead, she decided to stay home and bake a cake from scratch for Saturday night's dinner. She put some country music on the radio and danced around while she sifted the dry ingredients, boiled down the fruit, whipped the icing. She was throwing a dinner party. She was excited.

Lucy arrived at Hank's in the late afternoon with bags of groceries, flowers, wine, and a strawberry cream cake. Hank and Al and Big Mae were on the porch having a beer. It was a hot day. Lucy was wearing shorts. She had tried to flat iron her hair but the humidity was already making it frizz up and curl.

"That's a whole lot of food you got there, Luce," Hank said, as she was pulling the bags out of the car.

"Well, you could come and help me carry it in, honey," she said.

"Honey," Big Mae said, smiling, "isn't that nice?" Hank winced.

" Junior's in town getting more beer but he'll be back real soon," Al said. "Hanker, go help your girl with those bags," but Big Mae had already taken them.

Once inside, Big Mae helped Lucy unpack the groceries. At first she was surprised that this would be Hank's girlfriend: in looks and figure, Lucy was a lot more like Big Mae than any of the girls Hank usually went with. And then as soon as she thought that, she got it. Maybe Hank wasn't such a wanker after all.

"Welcome to the family, honey," she said to Lucy.

"Thank you," Lucy said, wondering how Hank's sister-in-law could tolerate being called Big Mae. She saw the physical similarities between them and wondered if Hank called her Big Lucy behind her back. But Hank didn't talk to anyone in Waterville except her. Then she remembered that there was also a daughter, also named Mae, who Hank called Maybelle, but was probably Little Mae. It settled her a bit.

"I'm so sorry about Al," Lucy said.

"Well, we just try to enjoy everyday. Now look at that gorgeous cake: when did they open a fancy bakery in Waterville?"

"I made it."

"You made it? Why, what a wonder! It smells delicious."

Lucy smiled. It was nice to have someone appreciate her cake, especially someone who was as good a baker as Big Mae obviously was. Even though Lucy hadn't tasted her cinnamon buns, they had looked and smelled delicious.

Hank and Al came into the kitchen. Al was so thin, so weak, and it made Lucy want to feed him right then and there.

"This is going to be so much fun," Lucy said, "And I have all kinds of things to make a wonderful dinner! Steaks and potatoes with butter and sour cream and . . ."

"Easy does it, ok?" Hank said.

Just then a horn honked in the driveway. Al Junior was back.

"Maybe he needs help carrying in the beer," Big Mae said. "Hank, can you go help Junior?"

"He doesn't need my help," Hank said because Junior walked into the house with a beautiful girl.

Junior was all smiles. "Miss Lucy, this here's Julianne."

"Nice to meet you," Lucy said.

"Nice to meet you, too," Julianne said.

"Well, well, well," Al said. "Miss Julianne. Glad you could join us." Hank looked Julianne up and down and then shot Junior a look that said, *you're an idiot.* Lucy didn't know who this girl was but she knew Hank: he hated having strangers in his house.

"We got enough for one more?" Junior asked.

"Sure," Lucy said, but who was this girl? Junior didn't introduce her to Hank or Big Mae—obviously, Al knew her. But she hadn't come with them from Miami. And Junior didn't grow up here.

Whoever she was, she looked more Miami than Waterville. In fact, she looked like that actress from that Miami spy show that Hank loved. Lucy couldn't remember what the show was called because she never really paid much attention to it even though it was Hank's favorite. He loved that girl. She was a spy who could make bombs, blow things up. She loved to shoot people. Lucy thought it was ridiculous but Hank taped the show on Thursday nights while he was watching it so he could watch it again on Fridays and when Lucy showed up on Saturday, they watched it then, too. The character's name was Fiona. That Lucy remembered because when she came on the screen, Hank would take a big breath and say the name, Fiona. "Gorgeous girl, isn't she?" he'd say to Lucy, every time, then he'd smile at Lucy, as though they were complicit in the observation and the longing. Yes, the actress who played Fiona was a gorgeous girl. A gorgeous girl on TV, who loved to shoot people. Julianne looked just like that girl.

But Lucy could see that Hank was annoyed. He had his arms crossed over his chest and he was shaking his head.

"We have plenty of food here," Big Mae said, "but you sure don't look like you eat much, Sugar."

"Oh, she can eat a lot," Junior said. "We just came from Denny's. This girl ate a Grand Slam, and a then a grilled cheese sandwich and fries. She sure loves her food."

Julianne just smiled. She wasn't embarrassed the way Lucy would have been if someone had said something like that about her. One weekend last fall, Hank took Lucy camping in the woods about twenty miles from Waterville. He said he needed to get out of town. Lucy wondered why he just didn't go by himself but then she knew. What if something happened? What if he got those pains in his chest?

They stayed for three days and Lucy had packed up enough groceries to cook all their meals. The first morning, she was frying bacon and eggs in a cast iron skillet over a campfire Hank had made and everything about the moment

—coming out of sleep into the cool air, the deep yellow and orange canopy of fall leaves, the crackling of the eggs, the glorious smell of bacon—made her happier than she had remembered being in such a long time. She'd said, "this is so wonderful. And breakfast is my favorite meal." Hank had looked at her and said, "How can you tell?" as if that was a joke.

Julianne was still smiling. That's skinny girls for you, Lucy thought. What's to be embarrassed about if you can eat all you want and never have it show?

"How'd that happen?" Hank wanted to know.

"How'd what happen, Wanker? Eatin' a grilled cheese?"

"No, Denny's," Hank said.

"Well, I got the beer and then I got hungry and thought well, hell, I wonder what Julianne is doing. What's the point of getting a phone number if you don't use it, right? Turns out she's off today so after lunch, I just said c'mon over for supper. Who woulda thunk it?" When Junior said this, in an exaggerated country and western voice that Lucy thought sounded kind of stupid, he was smirking and staring at Hank.

"You're an ass," Hank said.

"Takes one to know one," Junior said.

Then Big Mae said, very quickly, "let's get these groceries put away before all this food goes bad."

"Oh, it'll be ok," Lucy said. Something was happening here but she didn't know what it was.

Al said, "Junior."

Junior said, "Hey, the girl needs to eat. Needs calories back, especially after all that dancing."

"Jesus Christ," Hank said.

"Oh, are you a dancer?" Lucy asked. Julianne looked like a dancer, long and lithe and graceful. She was even wearing what looked like a leotard, with spaghetti straps, and a denim mini skirt.

"Me? Noooo," Julianne said, laughing. "I wish. I can hardly touch my toes."

"You sure danced up a storm last night, Party Girl," Junior said.

Oh, Lucy thought. Of course. They were at Sandalinis. She wondered what Hank did while they were there. Probably watched TV. Or maybe even caught up on his sleep.

"Junior?" Al said, and it was a warning, not a question.

"Well, I had a good partner," Julianne said, "made it easy."

"For an old man," Junior said, and he began putting the beers in the refrigerator.

"Noooo," Julianne said.

Hank turned and was heading for the front door. Lucy knew he was mad. On the few occasions when she'd suggested having some of her teacher friends over with their husbands, he'd said no. Hadn't even made an attempt at making excuses or giving explanations. He didn't like parties. He did not like people he didn't know in his house. He didn't even seem to want his own family to be there. Lucy thought Hank would have at least liked Julianne because she looked like Fiona but he only seemed angry that she was there.

"Age is just a state of mind," Al said, shaking his head. "You're as young as you feel. And I feel like having a beer. Now, how's about you old kids come join me and Hank on the porch. Bring some of them fancy beers you bought, Junior."

Lucy and Big Mae resumed unpacking the groceries.

"Steaks are beautiful," Big Mae said, though her voice had lost some of its cheer. "Should I put them in the fridge?"

"I was going to marinate them," Lucy said, pulling a bottle of Italian salad dressing out of a bag. She really liked Big Mae, liked having her there, was hoping they were planning to stay for a while. She felt terrible that Al was so ill. But maybe not so ill? At least he could still dance.

"It's great that Al can dance, Mae," Lucy said. "When Hank told me he was sick, I assumed that meant . . ."

Big Mae glanced toward the porch. "Al can't dance, honey. Not no more. He used to kick up a storm but that cancer, well, it's worn him out and one of his legs don't really work right. But he's been wanting to go almost everywhere he's ever been and up here, that means Sanadlini's."

"I'm sorry," Lucy said. "Did you guys have fun?"

"Yeah. Al loves that old place," Big Mae said. "He was tapping his cane on the ground like it was a third leg, he was singing to the oldies. It was a lot of fun for him."

"So no pizza, eh?' Lucy said.

"Oh, no, we had pizza. Their pizza's pretty good there."

"Oh. I meant here. Hank said you all were having pizza here last night. I thought maybe you did before you and Al and Junior went to Sandalini's."

Big Mae stopped organizing the groceries on the counter and it looked like she was thinking about something, trying to decide what to do next.

"Al, he made Hank come with us. You know, it's hard to say no to a guy who's dying, especially when it's your big brother."

Lucy nodded her head. Hank at Sandalini's? He must have been miserable.

So Al wasn't the "old man" Julianne danced with. It made Lucy laugh a bit inside to think that Julianne, who was obviously in her early twenties, would think Junior was old in his thirties. Maybe that's why Hank called Junior an ass. Hank thought dancing, especially men dancing on a dance floor, was the stupidest thing on earth. And Hank must have thought his nephew was really pushing it by bringing Julianne here. Hank hated when people embarrassed themselves, as Junior was doing by thinking he had a chance with this young girl. Lucy remembered how when she was in her twenties, she and all her friends thought anyone over thirty was old. People in their forties were really old.

People in their fifties were ancient.

Lucy opened the jar of Italian dressing and set about marinating the steaks.

At dinner, they all sat down at the big oak table that Hank and Al had eaten dinner at every night when they were growing up; it was an antique and Lucy knew that when Hank sold the house, he thought he could get a good price for the table, too. He'd told her that many times. Big Mae and Lucy put steaks and potatoes and salad and corn on the cob and garlic bread on dinner plates and Julianne, who wanted to help, set a full plate down in front of each person.

Junior sat between his father and Julianne. He looked smug, Lucy thought, and she felt a little sorry for him. He was a good-looking guy but he dressed like a farmer, which was odd since Lucy knew from Big Mae that he made a lot of money running the family car dealerships in Miami. Lucy had been to Miami once and it was like being in a movie. Everyone was so beautiful. Maybe Junior wore a suit to work, Lucy thought.

When Julianne dug in and said how delicious everything was, Junior put his arm around her and then rubbed her back but she didn't seem to notice, she was so intent on eating. It made Lucy envious and self-conscious, though also proud. It had been a very long time since she had cooked for this many people.

Hank ate heartily, too. With a lot more gusto than usual.

"Everything all right?" Lucy asked Hank, because she was surprised by how happy he suddenly looked. Hank was not a big smiler. But now he seemed actually to be enjoying himself and Lucy was ecstatic because she knew she was making him proud.

"Sure, Luce. Good food, by the way."

"Great food, Lucy," Junior said. "Eat up, Hankers. You need to keep your strength up, old man."

Hank picked up his ear of corn and tipped it toward Junior as if it was a hat.

"Don't mind if I do, bubba."

"How you doin' honey?" Big Mae asked Al. She could see he was having some trouble swallowing.

"A-OK, honey," he said. "You're some cook, Miss Lucy. This here's a great dinner and I'm just taking my time to enjoy every single bite."

"Well, I'm glad you didn't have steaks last night at Sandalini's," Lucy said. "They have great steaks there and I wouldn't want the competition."

"No contest," Junior said. "No competition at all." Then Junior shook his head, started laughing, had to put his fork down. "Sorry, Lucy," he said.

"About what?" Lucy asked. He had just given her a compliment that he seemed to be apologizing for.

"That you couldn't join us," Junior said, recovering. He was smiling at her in a way she couldn't interpret but did recognize. It was the kind of smile that said *I'm sorry but I can't help myself.* She didn't understand it. But every family had its own dynamic and she didn't really know Hank's so she just pushed on.

"Oh, well, no I couldn't." Lucy didn't want to say she hadn't been invited. "But it was fun, huh?"

"Do we have to talk about that place while we're having this great dinner here?" Hank said. Lucy watched him look at his brother for confirmation but Al's eyes were closed. Then Hank looked at Big Mae but she just patted Al on the shoulder and continued to eat. She was used to this, Lucy thought. It was incredibly sad.

"We had the best time," Julianne said. Lucy tensed up, hoping Hank wouldn't embarrass Julianne by reminding her that he'd just said no one should talk about Sandalini's.

"I love that place," Julianne went on. "It's so pretty inside, the way they have it fixed up. And they have the best food, especially the pasta. I had the Fettuccine Alfredo with Shrimp. It's so yummy."

"Uncle Hank thinks it's the tackiest place on earth," Junior said. "He hates it there."

"You do?" Julianne said, with genuine surprise. She looked over at Hank, who was staring at her.

"He's just fooling around," Hank said.

"Who's foolin' who?" Junior said. "Oh, baby, you don't know the half of it."

No doubt about it. Something was going on here but Lucy didn't know what it was. All she knew was that she wanted it to stop because it was making her uncomfortable. The dinner party had gone from fun to tense in a flash. Al seemed to be asleep and Big Mae had gone too quiet. Lucy was nervous but she was also proud of her dinner and she didn't want anything to go wrong.

"How did you guys all meet?" she asked Julianne. Change the subject. Get everyone back on track. It was a trick she used in her third grade class, when the kids started to get on each other's nerves.

"At the bar," Julianne said. "My girlfriends and I were having some more drinks after dinner, waiting for the band to start up, and this guy here, he sent over a round."

Which guy? Julianne was eating her corn on the cob with both hands and didn't gesture to who she meant.

Lucy looked at Hank and he was looking back at her now, shaking his head as if to say, *what a ridiculous girl. I had nothing to do with it*, which was how she suddenly knew he did.

"And then another round, after that," Junior said.

Lucy was middle-aged and overweight. Her glory days were long gone. She was good at being good, at getting along. It was how she liked to live her life. She liked taking care of people—the children in her class, her friends when they were troubled, Hank. Sometimes at home, before she fell asleep, she actually found it amusing that Hank thought he was fooling her. That he really didn't know that she knew exactly what was going on, why she was in his life. What was funny was the part he couldn't see, that she was using him, too. That they needed each other for different reasons and that for as long as it lasted, they were both getting what they needed out of it. He wasn't fooling her. But making a fool of her? That was something entirely different.

"Next thing you know," Julianne said, "we're all dancing." Then she stopped and looking at Al, said, "well, not all, I guess, but everyone was having fun."

Lucy put her knife and fork down.

"I love to dance," Lucy said. "People used to say I was good at it. Did you dance, Mae?" Lucy could see that Big Mae was the kind of woman who liked to dance.

"Sure she did," Julianne said. "Cut in on me and Hank a few times, which was good because I got to sit a few out. That cousin of yours, he wore me out."

Corn came flying out of Junior's mouth.

"Cousin?" he said, choking a little. "That's the best you could come up with? Jesus."

"Aren't you all cousins?" Julianne asked.

"Where'd you hear that, honey?" Al, whose eyes were open wide now, wanted to know.

"Hank told me, when we were coming in for dinner. I thought Lucy was his girlfriend but then he set me straight and told me Lucy was his cousin, your cousin, how you guys all grew up here together."

Lucy surprised herself. She laughed out loud.

"Didn't you?" Julianne asked.

"Sure we did," Lucy said. "Went to the same high school and everything."

Lucy had brought a carton of fresh strawberries and a can of whipped cream to decorate her strawberry cream cake. There were some options here. Confront Hank in front of everyone. Grab her purse and storm out of the house. Go to the bathroom and sneak out of the house. Put the dessert together and then figure out which one was the best choice. She was proud of the cake. It looked store-bought.

Julianne asked if she could help. Big Mae said no but Lucy said yes: she could clear the table. While Julianne brought the dinner dishes to the sink, Lucy cut the strawberries. She was tapping her foot as if there was music in her head. Every so often she looked up at Hank. He sat at the table staring at the space where his plate had been. *Look at me, you coward.* Big Mae took Al to the bathroom while Junior was in the living room, fiddling around with the stereo system, trying to find some music. He was definitely in the party mood.

Big Mae came back into the kitchen and whispered to Lucy, "You ok, hon?"

Lucy put her finger up to her lips. She was still trying to figure that out.

Big Mae rubbed Lucy's back. "Should I cut the cake?"

Lucy nodded. She pulled the dessert plates from one of the open shelves. She hadn't thought about it before but Hank had a fully equipped kitchen. He was a guy who didn't cook, never had guests, but obviously he had some even bigger plans than Lucy had understood. He had a full set of dessert plates. A state-of-the-art food processor, a blender, espresso machine and demitasse cups, champagne flutes. Six Danish barstools. Screwed to the wall under the shelving was a metal plate and from it hung expensive gadgets: apple corer, garnish knife, zester. Lucy thought they were Swedish. She didn't know why she had never really noticed these things before. She'd never needed them.

"Are there dessert forks?" Julianne asked. She had put all the dinner forks into the dishwasher.

Lucy looked around the kitchen as if it was her first time there. "I'm sure there are," she said and pulled open a drawer. Dishtowels. She pulled open another. Barbecue tools. The third one she tried contained a full set of pearl-handled dessert forks. And the gun.

Julianne was standing next to her. In a matter of seconds, Lucy could shoot her. Right between the eyes. She took the forks out, fingered the handle of the gun.

"Look at how gorgeous this cake cuts," Big Mae said. She began placing a thick slice of cake on each plate.

"Should I serve it?" Julianne walked up to Lucy just as she was closing the drawer. Lucy gave her the forks and said "You'd better."

Big Mae asked Al if he wanted coffee but Al said no, maybe another beer later. Hank was folding his linen napkin into a triangle, then unfolding it and refolding it again. He was tapping one foot fast on the floor but it was not to keep a beat. It was not dancing. Lucy thought he looked like he wanted to get up. Like he was ready to leave.

Julianne set a piece of cake down in front of each person. Hank who didn't eat dessert started eating his cake with his head down so low that any lower his face would have been in the whipped cream. From the counter, Lucy watched him.

"I love cake," Julianne said, swallowing a big bite. "I wish I could bake. But boy if I did, I'd be big as a house."

"Oh, there's time for that," Lucy said, remembering her skinny high school self. "But then again, not as much time as you'd think." The gun in the drawer gave the notion of time an entirely new perspective.

"Yeah, I know. My mom? She was as skinny as me when she was young but now, whoa. She can't even believe how fat she is. But it's from being a mom, you know? I have three brothers." Julianne was oblivious and if she would stop talking for five minutes, she'd be easier to ignore.

"I'm living proof," Big Mae said. "Kids make you fat."

"Me, too," Lucy said.

"How many kids do you have, Lucy?" Julianne asked.

"Dozens of them," and when poor Julianne looked confused, Lucy said, "I teach third grade."

Julianne started laughing. She thought it was a funny joke.

"But none of my own," Lucy went on. "Life doesn't always turn out the way you think it will." Proximity to the gun made Lucy bold. It made her patient and she felt wise. She was not young but she had been young once and for a long time after she had been, if not happy, content with how her life turned out. Not exactly how she thought it would but ok all the same. More times than not, it was actually pretty fine. And fine turned into predictable and predictable was safe and safe was the thing that kept you from getting hurt.

"That's for damn sure," Big Mae said. "Life sure throws you some surprises." She looked at Al and he winked at her. Then he turned his gaze back to his brother. He looked like he was about to say something but then Julianne broke in.

"I'm going to have a ton of kids," she said. "My boyfriend? He's in Iraq now and I was telling Junior at lunch that he's coming home for good in two weeks. Two weeks! Can you believe it? We're going to get married next year. He has a huge family—seven brothers and sisters. We're going to have so many kids, like maybe eight. Or ten. I can't wait. And I'll be fat and happy and running around in my pajamas chasing them all down."

Lucy watched Hank shift in his seat. She wondered what the solider boyfriend would do when he found out this old man was trying to pick up his girlfriend. She wondered what Fiona would do if her boyfriend was trying to pick up someone else's girlfriend. She'd shoot him.

"And maybe we'll have a house like this one someday," Julianne went on. "With lots of rooms and cool stuff and lots of land for the kids. I'd love my kids to live in a place like this. All this land. They'd love it."

"Maybe Hank'll sell it to you," Junior said.

No one said anything. Julianne because her mouth was full of cake. Everyone else was just waiting. No one seemed to notice that Lucy hadn't joined them at the table, that she wasn't having any cake. That she was just leaning on the counter with her hand on the dessert fork drawer.

"You're so lucky, Hank," Julianne said, "that you got to grow up here, and that you get to live here now. Cody would love it here."

"Oh, Hank's not too happy to be living here," Junior said.

"Shut up, Junior," Hank said. But Lucy could see that Junior was just getting started.

"Nope, not happy about living out here at all." Junior finished his cake and got to work on his father's uneaten slice.

"Yeah, I know," Julianne said. "Last night, Hank was saying it was pretty lonely out here for him." She looked over at Hank with sympathy.

"Lonely," Lucy said. "Being out here by himself all the time . . . except when us cousins visit."

"Did you ever visit him in Colorado?" Julianne asked.

"Oh, we were never invited to Uncle Hank's in Colorado," Junior said.

"What?" Julianne asked, and then she turned to Hank and laughing said, "you invited me out there last night!"

"Well, you know . . ." Junior wiped some cream off his lips with his hand. "You can take the hick out of Waterville but you can't take the Waterville out of the hick. We wouldn't make good company in Colorado, I guess. Maybe we don't have the right clothes."

"What?" Julianne didn't get it. Lucy did.

"Cody. Is that your boyfriend's name?" Lucy asked. Although she couldn't have cared less, she wanted to hear more about Julianne's boyfriend now.

"Yeah," Julianne said. "Are you ok?" Lucy had moved her hand from the drawer and now had both palms against the island, the granite island with the built-in wine refrigerator. Hank didn't drink wine. She was swaying, back and forth, lifting up one foot and then the other. Like she was getting ready to do something and, yet, almost like she was dancing.

"Sure," Lucy said. "Tell us more about Cody. What's he like?" Lucy wondered if she could shoot Hank. She was ready to do it, to open the drawer, pull out the gun, and shoot him in the chest, in the place where his heart was supposed to be. But she knew that would kill him immediately. That it would hurt less than what she was doing now.

"Oh, he's amazing. I can't wait until he gets home. He's really cute, you wouldn't believe it. He's really tall and he works out all the time so he's in great shape. Well, you have to be to be in the army. And he loves to hunt and fish and stuff. He works on cars, too. He'll work with his dad at their garage when he gets back. He's really smart. I mean not like school smart but smart like in life. You know what I mean?"

"Sure do," Junior said. "You know what she means, don't you Uncle Hank?"

Lucy looked at Junior and shook her head.

"You're pretty smart, too, Junior," Lucy said.

"Sorry, Lucy," Junior said, and she knew he meant it. "War has casualties."

"And heroes," Lucy said. The music Junior had put on was nothing she recognized but it had a good beat. Lucy used to love to do the Four Corners and The Hitchhiker, dances she and her friends had watched on television. When they were girls. And then she had a revelation.

"Junior?" she asked, "Why didn't your sister come? Little Mae? Maybelle?"

"Why don't you ask Hank?" he said.

"How the hell should I know?" Hank said. His voice cracked when he said it, like he was having trouble getting the air to talk. He looked at Lucy but she looked away.

"You know," Junior said. "Because you know Little Mae. You know how she is. If you wanted her to come, you should have . . ."

"She had to work," Big Mae cut in. "We told you that, Hank."

"No she didn't," Lucy said, completely sure of herself though since she had never behaved like this, she wasn't exactly sure who she was. But she liked this new person, the one with guts. "She didn't want to come. Why not?"

"No, no," Big Mae said, "she did," but she wasn't telling the truth.

"Let's just let it out now," Junior said. "It's because when Mamma called Hank to tell him Daddy was sick, Hank hung up and never called back. Little Mae hates his gutless guts now."

Hank looked at Lucy again. He wanted her to help him, like she always did. She wanted to break out from behind the island and start doing The Twist. That would kill him, she thought.

"See, old Hankers doesn't like a mess. He likes nice things, right? Look at all the things he's got here. And he likes money. Daddy'll be leaving him some money. But he don't like to get in the mess first."

"It's not like . . ." Hank stopped in mid-sentence.

"Cat got your tongue, Wanker?" Junior asked. "Want to talk to Daddy now?"

"Stop it, Junior," Al said. "This isn't your business. I know my brother. Everyone handles things differently. We're here now. It was the right thing. It's enough."

"It's not enough, Daddy," Junior said. "We're here because you wanted to come here but it's not enough for you. It's not good enough for you. How can you still care about this asshole?"

"Junior!" Big Mae said. "Now that is enough."

But Lucy thought Junior was right. It wasn't enough. She knew Hank cared more about himself than anyone else but she thought he loved his brother. Maybe that was why he couldn't talk to him when he got sick. It made him sick. And Lucy could see he was sick now.

She could help him because she was there but being there would never be enough because it didn't matter. Being gone wouldn't matter. She picked her purse up from the counter, pulled her car keys out of it. She had brought her overnight bag because it was Saturday but because there were so many bags of groceries to carry in, she had—blessedly—left it in her car.

Fiona would have left a long time ago, blood in her wake. The show was called *Burn Notice*. The name suddenly came into Lucy's mind. Fiona could shoot anyone. That was her answer to everything bad that happened. It was a big part of what made her so charming. The bravery, the impulsiveness. Extraordinarily beautiful girl who has no problem shooting people. Who could do it and walk away.

"Maybe I should go?" Julianne asked. Lucy knew even someone as dumb as Julianne could see something terrible was happening. "I'm sorry and the dinner was great and everything but I think really if like Junior you wouldn't mind taking me home because I have to . . ."

"Shut up," Hank said. Lucy could see he wanted to stand up but he had that look on his face she knew, the one that said he had pains in his chest.

"Lucy?" he said.

"Shut up."

Shut up is something Lucy knew Fiona would say to this man begging her to save his life. She would shoot him. And then make herself an espresso in his never-been-used espresso machine.

"I'll take you home, Julianne," Lucy said. It was the least she could do.

The Hungry Girl

He does not recognize me.

He walks into the room nonchalantly, as if he is just stopping by. He greets me first only because I am seated closest to the door, and mine is the first face he sees. He takes my hand and says, "Bonjour. Je suis Chef Yves" because he thinks he is a charming Frenchman and that he owes all women the opportunity to swoon.

"I'm Veronica," I say. "You don't remember me, but I was here last summer, too."

"Oui, oui, of course," he says. "Veronique. Lovely to see you again."

He is not French. He studied cooking in Paris and he knows some French words but he was born and raised in Indiana. I know this because I have Googled him, studied him, as if he was a report I had to do for school. His real name is Evan Pearlman. He combs thin strands of hair over his bald spot. He wears loafers without socks. And a gold chain around his neck. He is fat. But I cannot dwell on any of this right now because I have spent the last year trying to be lovely to be seen again, trying to become Veronique.

He sits down and his assistant, Delia, walks into the room and sits down beside him. She sees me and says, "Veronica, you're back! You look fantastic."

Now Chef Yves looks at me again, trying to see if Delia is right.

This is a Food Safety Certification course and Chef Yves teaches it because he is too washed up to do anything else in the culinary world. Last year he almost went to jail but he got lucky and then luckier when this hotel, the scene of his crime, decided he could come back again to teach the course this year. I don't understand that but I'm very happy about it. Makes everything so much easier for me.

Chef's idea of teaching is useless for anyone who needs to learn the essentials, which presumably we all do, because he spends the bulk of the time talking about himself. But there is a manual and it provides all information necessary to pass the exam. More to the point, however, is the fact that Chef is responsible for grading the exam. Basically, if you put your name on it, you pass.

I failed the exam last summer by not taking it. That was not my original intention but in the end, I had no choice. I was at the police station when the exam was being given. And someone else graded it anyway because Chef was, also, otherwise occupied.

I don't really need the certification. Originally, I just wanted it for my back-up plan. I'm a private chef in a movie star's home on Fisher Island; last year, I had decided to take the exam because I was getting tired of the neuroses, the fad diets, of broiling chicken and serving it over the greens I had to convince my employer were not dressed, and I thought at some point she would drive me to move on to a kind of cooking that would be appreciated. I am only twenty-eight. There are lots of things in the food world left for me to do.

But the first one is to retake the certification class and make Chef Yves fall in love with me. I owe at least that much to Charlotte.

Charlotte. Charlotte Matthews, Chef's obsession from last year. She did not take the exam last summer either but she will not be returning. Ha! Sometimes I crack myself up. Last year, Chef didn't see anyone in the class except Charlotte. This year, I am the prettiest girl. Even though he doesn't exactly see me.

He introduces himself in the same long and windy way he did last year and then asks everyone in the class to state their name, occupation, and where they will be staying during the week long course.

"In case I need to see you," he says, "or if we have a change in plans and I need to get in touch with you."

You mean touch you, don't you Chef, I want to say, to remind him of what got him into so much trouble last summer. But in this past year where I never touched a carbohydrate, woke up two hours early to run and then swim in my movie star's lap pool, taught myself how to wax my own eyebrows and high-light my own hair, I have learned a kind of patience that prevents me from acting on any of my impulses. The two men in the class are staying in their own homes in Miami. The three other women are staying down the road at the Comfort Inn. Though I only live two miles away in a condo I own, I am stay-ing in this expensive hotel where the class is being held.

"Tres bien," Chef says. "Let's get started."

Getting started means we students read silently to ourselves from the in-troduction to the manual and then just before lunch, we will have a chance to ask questions.

I don't have any questions.

Last summer I ate all my meals in the hotel's dining room and I eat my lunch there today. The waiters work double shifts to ensure the continuity of the guests' dining experience since on any given day, many eat lunch and din-ner there. Chef Yves claims he has known the chef here for years and that he is a fraud. He tells the class this as if it is a secret we are all going to share. I order the Caesar Salad. And a bowl of fresh strawberries in a balsamic glaze. Both are fine, good even, but I am wearing my chef coat and tell the waiter I find the salad watery and the berries sour. He apologizes and says the chef would like to take care of my bill.

After lunch, we all file back into the conference room and Chef begins to tell us why Food Safety is so important.

"Because you need to keep your customers safe. Because you need to not kill your customers with your food. Because if you work in a restaurant, the Health Department will come when you don't expect them and shut you down if your kitchen is not up to code."

Chef knows a lot about this. He owned Bistro Yves for three years before the Health Department showed up when he didn't expect them and shut his restaurant down because his kitchen was not up to code.

"How many of you work in a restaurant?"

Everyone except me raises their hand.

"You, pretty girl in the front here, where do you work?"

Pretty girl. See? That is me now. "In a private residence, on Fisher Island," I say.

"Ah, so you can kill your clients if you want and no one will come after you." Chef Yves thinks he is a comedian.

"Except the movie-going public," I say.

I say this on purpose. Chef Yves loves famous people. He namedrops all the time.

"Who is it that you cook for?" he asks.

"I'm sorry but I'm not allowed to say."

This is not true. I've told tons of people who I cook for.

"Where are you staying again?' he asks. "In case I need to be in touch with you."

Right I think and say, "Right here."

Charlotte was two girls. She was the really beautiful girl who flirted with the teacher. She was the bitchy girl who mocked him behind his back. Both of those girls got exactly what they wanted but neither got what they deserved.

I am two girls now too and when I arrive to meet Chef for dinner in the dining room at 8:00, I request the same waiter I had at lunch. This time I am wearing a black sheath, V-neck, tight.

"Nice to see you again, Chef," the waiter says to me.

"Likewise," I reply. "Long day for you."

"Yes, thank you. What can I get you to drink?"

I order a glass of Sancerre.

Chef arrives at 8:15. He is wearing a purple silk shirt and there are large sweat stains under his arms. The bald spot on his head is glistening. When he sits down, he takes my hand and his palm is wet. I kind of want to throw up.

"You look beautiful," he says.

I smile and nod my head, as if stating the obvious does not require a response with words.

"You are having vin?" Again, with the obvious, though this time partly in French. I play along.

"Oui," I reply. "A French Sancerre."

"Tres bien," he says. "An excellent wine. The Sancerre has notes of . . ."

This would be excruciating if it wasn't so much fun. If I didn't have a plan. I've got to give my famous actress employer some credit here, too; I've learned some important things working for her. I am the master of not revealing what I am really thinking because I must always convince her that I take her neuroses seriously, that I am not at all bothered when she calls me in the middle of the night because she has friends over and they are hungry, that I have no life and no other purpose in my non-existent life other than to serve her, to please her, to make everything all right. I am practiced in how not to let people know how absurd I find them. I could be an actress, too.

But I do wish Charlotte was here. At this table or even across the room, maybe in a disguise. We could do this together. I think she would love it.

I ask Chef if he would like a glass of the Sancerre. I do not tell him that the chocolate notes he claims are in this wine do not exist.

An hour into our dinner, we are half way through a second bottle of the Sancerre and a platter of oysters on the half shell and Chef has talked non-stop about Cat Cora, the famous and only female Iron Chef. He claims they are friends, that he taught her how to cook, that they were "involved" in their youth.

Chef does not know that Cat Cora is my all-time favorite chef. Or that I aspire to be just like her. Or that she is a lesbian. I say, "I love Chef Cora" and Chef thinks I am kissing up to him. He likes it.

"But you are so much prettier than she is," he says.

Please.

He tells me more stories about Chef Cora, how they fell in love, how the relationship was doomed. He is lying to impress me and because he thinks I know nothing and I sit here wondering how it is possible that he knows less than nothing. Cat Cora has four children with her wife. She is a great chef and seems really nice. I know that even if she were straight, she would never go for a guy like Chef. Obviously, Chef does not know that Cat Cora is gay but he assumes we are all beneath him, that none of us students knows what he knows, that we will believe whatever he says, whatever he invents in his enormous head. It is entertaining.

Chef has told the waiter, in no uncertain terms, that we want to take our time so while he rambles on about how Cat Cora knew nothing about spice blends until he came along, we are waiting for our next course, Caesar salad.

When the waiter sets the salads down, he says to me, "the Chef hopes this is more to your liking, Chef," and I say thank you. Chef Yves becomes immediately and noticeably on edge.

"You have been here before?" he asks.

I wonder what would happen if I tried to wipe the sweat that is now dripping off his forehead. He would think I want to touch him. So instead, I say, "Many times."

"Ah, so you know them here?" I feel his foot tapping under the table. This is hilarious.

"Oui."

Chef is becoming afraid of me. Things are going even better than I had planned. Now he fears that I might discover that he does not know the chef here at this restaurant. And he thinks I do.

"You do as well, right?" I say, in the high voice of the practiced sychophant. "You know the chef here?"

"Well, the chef here, it turns out, is now a different one. Not the one I knew from before. I, uh, I just learn this today."

Sometimes when Chef speaks, he uses English the way foreigners do.

"Oh," I say, and delicately fork a piece of lettuce. I place it in my mouth. "Magnifique," I say.

We have not ordered our entrees yet. Chef says it is better to have the salad first, then decide what your palate craves, as if his students—who are also chefs —don't know how to eat. My palate craves a pizza from Room Service in my bed watching *Law and Order* reruns but I will order the lobster because I know Chef cannot afford to pay this bill. I know all about his financial situation. It's why he is back here, teaching this course. I want to see his face when I order the lobster. I will eat only two bites, feign fullness, and order the pizza when I finally get back to my room. Once my work here is done, I will definitely deserve some fat and carbs.

During the salad course, Chef continues talking about his famous chef friends—Bourdain, Zakarian, Morimoto. Not that I doubted it before but now I am even more certain that he does not remember me from last summer because he spent one whole class then telling these same exact stories. What is even funnier is that these are famous stories about these famous chefs, apocryphal tales that are legend in foodie circles. Everyone knows them. That's why Chef knows them. But then he appropriates them and puts himself at the center of them because like all bad teachers, he assumes we will believe anything he says. I have a brief moment where I want to tell him that Chef Cat Cora is my mother.

But I refrain. As he drones on, I contemplate my next move. Chef is here, he has asked me to join him for dinner, because he has not learned his lesson. I counted on this and it came true. He is here because he is vain and self-important. Because when he looks in the mirror, he does not see how he has aged. He is that kind of man. Because the hotel agreeing to let him return here to teach the course again after what he did last summer has obviously allowed his bluster to overcome his memory. He sees me as someone he thinks he can impress and manipulate. He sees someone he thinks he can sleep with. If he only knew.

I ask him how he thinks the first day of class went, what he thinks of the students. He flicks his hand as if he thinks they are all gnats.

"These people," he says, "why are they here? What is that they need to know?"

"I am one of those people, Chef," I say.

"Oh no, I do not mean you. You are different, Cherie." He thinks I will be over-the-moon flattered that he wants me. He is sure I won't resist. But it doesn't really matter to him because he is not in love with me. That was the mistake he made with Charlotte Matthews.

The waiter reappears and asks what we would like for dinner. Chef tells him we will be splitting the Miso-Glazed Salmon but then I say, "Oh, no. I would like the Lobster, please."

Chef looks at me and says, "Really?" I say, "Bien sur."

"Very good, Chef," the waiter says to me. "Will you still be having the Salmon, sir?"

Chef Yves says, "Chef" and the waiter says, "Pardon?" and Chef Yves says, "I am a chef" and the waiter says, "Sorry, Sir, Chef. Will you still be having the Salmon?"

Chef Yves says "Oui" and as the waiter walks away, I know he is laughing.

"So your employer," Chef says. Ah, here we go. Chef cannot resist the rich and famous.

"Yes?" I say, as innocently as possible.

"Who is he, if I may ask. You can trust me."

"It's a she, actually," I say, "and yes, of course, I trust you but I'm sorry. I just cannot say."

"Oh, Cherie," he says, "truly, you may. I just ask you because I can help you . . . with her. I know many of the famous types, very well. And I can tell you are not happy."

Seriously? I am ecstatic.

"Is English your first language, Chef?" I ask, as if I must divert the conversation from my alleged unhappiness.

"Well, oui, yes, I mean yes it is but, you know? I have so much time in France, so much French, that sometimes I cannot tell the difference. You know?"

"I do," I say. "I know," and then, because I am starving and not sure if I can wait any longer, I say, "you really don't remember me, do you?"

"Of course I do," he says. "Bien sur."

"Who am I?"

"Why, you are Veronique."

"Yes, I am. I sat next to Charlotte last summer."

Here we go. Chef wants to use his hand to wipe the sweat off his neck but as he moves it too quickly from its position of trying to take my own hand, it knocks over his recently filled glass of Sancerre.

"Charlotte is insane," he says. "Crazy. Fou."

"Oh?" I say, "you've seen her?"

Our extremely conscientious waiter runs over and is dabbing the spilled wine from the table. Another waiter follows and refills Chef's glass. The service here is excellent.

"No, no, I have not seen her. I have not talked to her. Not since last summer. Not at all. But she was crazy, last summer, when I saw her."

In court? I want to ask but I don't because it is more fun watching him trying to figure out what I know, how much I heard, how well I know her. Who I am.

"She is married now," I say.

"What?" he says, clearly distressed. "Married? No, she is not."

"Yes, she is," I say, "to a famous television actor. They got married at Thanksgiving. In Vermont. I was in their wedding."

This is a total lie. All of it.

"Who?" he wants to know.

"Why, Charlotte," I say. I am having so much fun.

"No, I mean, what actor? What television actor is married to Charlotte?"

"Oh, I'm really not at liberty to say."

This shows you just how stupid Chef really is, how his madness over this news obliterates any sense he might have had. If Charlotte were married to a famous television actor, everyone would know. Hello, *People Magazine?*

"Oh, well," Chef says, trying to compose himself, "really? I did not know. So, uh, good, bon, good for her. She is married. That is good for her. She must live in L.A. then? With her famous actor? Or New York? She is in New York? She is happy, no?"

"She is happy, yes," I say. "But she would have been happier if you had gone to jail, you know."

Charlotte and I never spoke during class, although I always wanted to talk to her. We did sit next to each other but she never paid any attention to me. Never even said hello. I was heavy and quiet and not pretty. Chef completely ignored me, too, even when I raised my hand.

Charlotte was magical. She looked like a model. Her hair was blonde, down to her waist, and straight as a wall. She had an angelic face—all huge blue eyes, dark lashes, pink lips, blushed cheeks. Unreal. She was the kind of thin that you wanted to touch. She wore shorts and tank tops and wedge sandals that seemed impossible to walk on but Charlotte sort of floated. She crossed her legs with an ease I couldn't even imagine. I wanted to kiss her.

So did Chef. He was so stupid in love that he had no shame. He brought her gifts, nearly every day, like coffee and flowers and chocolates and once glittery hair clips (which was freaky and weird, though I got it since that hair was irresistible). He invited her to dinner, out loud, in front of the whole class. And she accepted. Every night.

Chef had no idea what a fool he was making out of himself. This is what a beautiful woman who doesn't care about other people's feelings can do to a man who can't see himself for what he is. On the second day of class, he wore cologne. He passed by Charlotte in the hallway before class started and I saw her pinch her nose. I was down the hall a bit, listening to her talk on the phone, telling someone—maybe her boyfriend—how ridiculous Chef was. But Chef didn't know it. He thought they were in love. When he got drunk the last night and forced his way into her hotel room and asked her to marry him and tried to kiss her and wouldn't take no for an answer and ripped her nightgown off and got on top of her, she screamed so loud that the person in the room next to hers called Security and then banged on Charlotte's door to cause a distraction until Security showed up.

That person was me.

"Jail? Jail? What . . . why . . . what are you talking about? Why would she want such a thing?"

"Because you are a rapist," I say, matter of factly. Even though there was a trial, Chef thought no one knew. A full courtroom with witnesses and reporters and observers but even then, Chef stared only at Charlotte so I guess he didn't realize how many of us were there.

"You are mistaken," he says to me.

Maybe it was because, in the end, Charlotte withdrew the charges that he thought it had gone away. Or never happened in the first place. I take a sip of my Sancerre, say "No, I'm not," and then scoot my chair back a tiny bit because out of the corner of my eye, I see my gigantic lobster arriving.

"Who are you?" Chef says. He is a different man now. The bravado is gone. So is the French accent. Now he is just angry.

"Chef, your lobster," the waiter says, and places it before me.

"That is beautiful," I say. "My compliments to the chef."

"Sir?" The waiter places the Salmon in front of Chef Yves.

"Bon appetit," the waiter says.

"Who are you?" Chef Yves asks me again. I take the first bite of my lobster.

"I am Veronique," I say. "You know that," and then I call him "Silly" be- cause I am having the time of my life. All these months of preparing but I never really knew I could be this girl. It is exhilarating.

"How dare you call me a rapist?" he says.

"Well, aren't you?" I say. I take a small piece of bread from the basket and dip it in the lobster butter. I am famished.

"I don't know what you heard but I did not rape that girl or anyone else. She was crazy. I didn't go near her."

"What?" I say. "You followed her everywhere. You went into her room." I really want to put the napkin in the collar of my dress and start to tear apart this lobster but I have waited so long and have to stick to my plan.

The waiter reappears and asks how everything is.

"I did not," Chef says, too loudly.

The waiter says "I'm sorry sir, The fish is not hot?" because that's what he heard and it distracts Chef from the problem of me. He is so furious. I feel bad for our waiter but there is little I can do now. I've come, or gone, too far.

"This salmon is cold . . . and overcooked." Both the waiter and I see that Chef has not taken a single bite and so could not know the temperature of the fish, or how it is cooked.

"So sorry, Sir. Would you like something else?"

"No. Yes. Wine. More wine."

"Are you sure, Chef?" I say. "Isn't that what got you in trouble last time?"

Why did Charlotte accept his dinner invitations? Maybe she was that bored. But mostly I think she wanted to pass the class without having to actually take the exam and she was the kind of girl who understood the power of her ap- peal. And she was special and she liked being special, being the person in the class everyone wanted to be. You could see it in the way she walked, and talked. You could also see she thought Chef was a doofus, that she was certain of her ability to get what she needed from him without any sacrifice except a bit of her time; after all, she had to be at the class all week. And she had to eat.

At the dinners, right here in this very restaurant, she talked and talked and talked about herself, her famous employer, the escapades of the house where she worked. Frankly, the stories bored me—I had much more dramatic ones in my own world. But she was charming and witty and so beautiful and she thought she had Chef wrapped around her little finger and Chef, who was wrapped around her little finger, somehow forgot who and what he really was and believed they had something special so neither one of them saw where they were heading. He paid for their lavish dinners, so many bottles of wine, with a credit card that I imagined he must have maxed out in that one week and I guess in addition to thinking they were in love, he thought he deserved something else for all the trouble he would have to face when the credit card bill came.

How do I know all this?

Because I ate dinner in the hotel dining room, too, at the table right behind theirs. Every night. The first time, it was just a coincidence but then it became purposeful. You might think that my being at my table every night before they arrived—that they would have seen me as they walked in—would have made them question what I was doing there, or at least say hello, but the great irony is the girl I was back then was not anyone that either of them ever saw. I sat close enough to them to hear all of their conversations. I was a giant invisible ear.

I took notes on my cocktail napkins. After they left, I went up to my room and went over my notes. I didn't know what I was going to do with them but they were the only notes I took all week and much more interesting than food safety certification. Chef's seduction was like a bad movie, Charlotte's responses were all masked in flirty laughter but I liked having the sound of her voice trapped in the words I wrote down.

I guess you could say it was an obsession, but you couldn't really say for what. Was I jealous? Was I in love? Was I just mad because I knew that if I jumped out of my hotel room window, no one in that class would have known I'd been in there? I don't know. But it doesn't matter because in the end, I was the hero.

"You really don't remember me, do you?" I say to Chef again because he is looking at me as if I am a total stranger and, despite my warning, the waiter has gone off to get his wine. I take the second bite of my lobster and then push it away. I have amazing will power now. It's astounding.

"You have the wrong information," he says to me. He sits back, tries to calm himself down, to reassume the authority he thought he had when he invited me to dinner.

"I was the one pounding on the door," I say.

I pounded and pounded and I know they heard me because I could hear Charlotte screaming "help me, help me" and then two Security officers arrived and one used a master key to open the door.

Chef had Charlotte pinned to the bed. Her nightgown was torn. Her breasts were exposed. They were nice, full but not too big. Chef had his big hand on one of them and I wanted to bite it off. Both officers pulled him off of Charlotte and I ran in to her. She sat up and threw her arms around my neck and I pulled what was left of her nightgown back up around her shoulders and rubbed her back. She was so thin, but her skin was warm and she held me so close I could feel her heart.

"I am here," I said to her then.

"I was there," I say to him now.

Chef is silent. The waiter brings a third bottle of wine and opens it. He fills Chef's glass and asks if we want dessert. Chef says no but I say yes and ask our waiter what he recommends. He says the passion fruit soufflé. This restaurant is famous for it.

"Perfect," I say.

Chef drinks his wine as if it is water.

"I was there," I say. Again. For dramatic effect.

And I see him, finally, seeing me. Remembering. Here I am, Chef. That girl from the front row. The girl whose name you could never recall, even though there were only five other people in the whole class. The girl who you never saw raising her hand because you was always looking at Charlotte. I was that fat girl in the sweatpants and Dolphins t-shirt who got to hold, to save, the thin quivering beautiful Charlotte as the security officers hauled you away. I was the shrinking girl in her chef whites testifying at your trial. I am the pretty girl sitting across from you now. The hungry girl.

Chef looks weary. Worn down. I would feel sorry for him if I wasn't the girl he invited to dinner. If he wasn't so stupid. If he wasn't that kind of man.

"What do you want?' he asks.

"To thank you," I say.

The waiter brings the soufflé. It is pink, bubbling and smells like heaven. But I push my chair back and stand up because it is time for me to leave.

"For what?" he asks.

"For giving me what I wanted. What I deserved."

Saving Julie

These two women do not know each other. They have never met. One is in her apartment, ear to the door, listening to the other one who is on the phone in the hallway.

The one in the apartment is Denise. She is mad. She lives across the hall from the combined laundry and trash room so she hears people coming and going all the time. But that's the point: coming and going. They always go. But this woman, Doreen, does not go. Instead, she leans on Denise's front door. And talks on her phone.

"And I told Julie . . . what? No, I'm not going to drink. I gained ten pounds from drinking and now I'm through. What? I know, I know . . . no, she's ridiculous. She even went to the fish market because she said 'Doreen, I know you like fish' and she said she's going to cook all day and then she said Andrew was coming and I was like, Andrew, oh God, and that is just going to be too weird. No, I didn't say that to her but I was thinking, God, I can't do this . . ."

Then please stop doing this, Denise thinks. She wants to open the door and tell her to go away. She has the right. But her desire for it to stop does not put her hand on the doorknob. She wants it to. She does not want to hear words and wishes it was just a blahblahblah of annoying amorphous white noise that would fade if she would just go back to her couch, turn up her TV. But what she hears instead is a woman she does not know but is starting to despise.

"Don't be ridiculous, Elaine. There is just no way in hell that I am going to do that. Andrew doesn't even know I know about her. But he's sure going to find out at some point because I am NOT going sit and there and be . . . what? Yes, of course, it will be horrible—dreadful—it's going to last forever . . ."

Nothing lasts forever. Denise doesn't understand why Doreen isn't moving, why it doesn't occur to her that her conversation is being overheard by people trying to live quietly in their apartments. She doesn't understand why Doreen is not talking loudly in her own apartment.

". . . and Julie'll probably wear one of those stupid outfits she has, matching shorts and shirt, oh God, I don't know."

Poor Julie. You just never know what people are saying behind your back. It makes it so much harder to live. Denise tries to look out of her peephole to get a glimpse of Doreen, see what she's wearing.

"This dinner is going to be a nightmare. I can't even believe I have to go and . . . yes, yes you are. You are definitely going because I am NOT going to this by myself."

But Andrew will be there. All Denise can see is an arm, thin, sleeveless. Doreen is leaning against Denise's front door, just to the side of the peep hole. Her voice is so forceful, it seems to barrel right through the door and wrap itself around Denise's head. From her style of talking, Denise thinks maybe Doreen is in her late 30s, and maybe from New York or Boston. She has some kind of an accent. Denise knows she could open her door and ask Doreen to, please, take this conversation somewhere else, but she is afraid if she does that, Doreen will fall backward right into her arms.

"Well, if Andrew brings that girl then it's going to be so weird and, you know, he doesn't even know I'm in town unless Julie told him. But it would be just like her to set this up, to set me up and humiliate me. What? How can I do that? I can't not go now that I said I was going. Who does that?"

A lot of people do that. I know it. People say yes and sure and love to right away when you ask and then days later call to say they're sorry, so sorry, but they can't come. Sometimes they do it on the day of your party. People do this. They do it all the time.

"She's lucky I even said yes. *Oh, lucky Julie.* No, no, I know, it's sad. OK? I admit that. All that seafood and she's spending all that money and it sucks because I made a pact with myself that I would hardly eat anything while I was down here because I've gotten so fat . . . oh, ok, fine, so not fat but fatter then I want to be so I don't even want to eat hardly anything and you know she's going to make potatoes and have cheese and dessert."

Well, of course she will. It's a dinner party. It has to have courses. Appetizers, side dishes, a beautiful dessert. What is wrong with that?

"No. Absolutely not. I am not calling Barb to see if she was invited. *Who's Barb?* You are. Will you? Thank you, thank you, thank you. You are saving my life."

Who's going to save Julie? Denise imagines her at the fish store, back home setting all her ingredients out, putting on some music to cook to, pouring a glass of good red wine, a more expensive one than she usually drinks because she is having company.

"That would be great, yes, pick me up. What time does it start? 6:00? Why 6:00, for God's sake, why so early? *6:00 is a normal time for a dinner party.* Shit. Are we going to have to stay there all night? No, but I have stuff I want to do today and I don't know how long it will take. What? Like work out and walk on the beach and get a mani-pedi *mani-pedi? Do people really say that?* at the Ritz—and I don't want to be rushed and also I don't want to get myself all ready just to sit in that house all night telling Julie how great her seafood is. *I can see how that would put you out.* What? No, it's not about Andrew. I don't care about Andrew. *Right.* God."

Denise's apartment building is across from the Ritz Carlton in South Beach. It's a building with local residents, like her, and one with lots of tourists, too, like Doreen. It's right on the beach. People rent their units out to vacationers, who are generally more rude than residents but in Denise's ten years here, no one has been as oblivious to the fact that people live behind the doors in these hallways, that some of them might even be home—that these apartments are their homes. Even the drunken college kids who come down on Spring Break whisper when they stumble in from the clubs at 5:00 a.m.

When Doreen is quiet, she's listening to Elaine but that doesn't last long.

"Well, I don't know. What difference does it make? Capris maybe, or a skirt. Who cares? *I do. I'm curious. What do people wear to parties they don't want to go to?* It's not like anyone who matters is going to be there. *What about Andrew?* I don't know. I don't why I said yes except she ambushed me with the invite, saying the dinner is all for me, my welcome dinner, and that's the thing, isn't it? I mean if someone says 'are you busy on Saturday' and you say no and then they say 'good, I'm having a dinner party for you and I'm making seafood because I know you love it' how do you say uh, no, I can't make it? I forgot I have plans. You can't do that."

Well, sure you can. You can say whatever you want. Isn't that what you're doing now? You could just save Julie from all that work, from the humiliation she doesn't even know about, from spending money she doesn't really have to make you feel welcome. You could stop her from meticulously following the recipes, moving furniture to make room for your friends, polishing her wine glasses. It's so much work to put on a dinner party. You want to think, you have to think, your guests want to come. Especially your guest of honor. You could save Julie's life.

"Who else do you think is going to be there? You can't even guess? No, no, I'm not yelling at you *yes you are* I'm just saying. I'm just asking. And how long do you think we have to stay there? Because if it's going to be an all-night thing, I'm going to die *you're going to die from being at a dinner party in your honor?* listening to her all night . . . 'Oh, Doreen, did I tell you about . . .' and 'Doreen, did you hear about Aunt Bette?' as if anyone cares about our crazy family. *Sometimes people like funny stories about other people's families. People used to crack up when I told the stories about my belly dancing cousin in Wyoming.* Ugh. But if we can go and stay for a little while and then go out after, that's different. And that will make a difference in what I wear. Because then I'm going to wear this dress I brought, little flowery thing. Sundress. Really cute. What? No, not that one. You haven't seen this one. It's new. But I've GOT to go get my shoulders tanned first."

Denise's neck is starting to hurt and she wishes she had a chair in the hallway so she could sit down. Julie and Doreen are probably cousins. And obviously Julie isn't included in Doreen's plans when Doreen comes to Miami Beach. Maybe Julie and Doreen's mothers are sisters and maybe Doreen's mother told Julie's mother Doreen was coming. Maybe Julie is a lot older than Doreen and doesn't fit in. Or maybe she's fat and would embarrass Doreen at a club.

"Just here, behind the building. You can rent chairs, or I'll just take a towel but I have GOT to get some sun before I go anywhere. I'm white as a ghost."

Denise would like to be a ghost. Then she could pass through her door and float around the hallway, get a good look at Doreen. If she were a ghost, she could yank Doreen's feet out from under her or pinch the skin under her arms or pull her hair.

"She's sleeping. *Who's sleeping?* No, she doesn't want to go at all and you know what? She might not even go. She wants to go to Prime 112. Have you been? When I was there last year I saw Dennis Rodman. *Big deal* Yeah, cool, I know. She says she can get us all in without a reservation. *Not unless she's Beyonce* I don't know! How should I know? No, I'm not going to tell her. Let her do what she wants. Who cares? No, she can't hear me; I'm in the hall way *oh . . . ok, I get it* I don't know. She can sleep a long time. I don't know how long she'll sleep."

Denise wants to know who is sleeping in the apartment, who is the cause of her discomfort. She doesn't know how long she'll stay here listening to this, though she has nothing else to do. Doreen is oblivious to Denise but Denise is hyper-aware of both of them. She wonders if her own little flowered sundress still fits.

She puts her television program on pause. Her own phone rings. She looks at the clock—10:50. Telemarketer. Or maybe someone from the Firefighters Fund or Leukemia Society asking for money. Denise always gives something. She likes to hear about the various causes, about people in need. She likes the grateful way the callers accept her donations. Doreen doesn't hear Denise's phone or if she does, it doesn't stop her.

"Ok, ok, this is what I'm going to do. I'm going to go to the gym here in the building and get a work out in. A big one. I need it. Then I'll go for a walk on the beach and get some sun. Shoulders need tanning, remember? Then I'll go to the Ritz salon. Then...I don't know. Maybe I'll walk up Lincoln Road and shop a little. Do you wanna come? I don't know. 2:00 or 3:00? What? Yeah, 4:00's ok...well, how about this? You come here at 4:00 and we'll go out and then we'll get a drink before we have to go over there. We'll need one. Especially if I have to pretend to eat all that food."

I bet you'd eat if Dennis Rodman took you to Prime 112. Denise knows Julie and is sure she would really like her. She knows Julie must be someone without any real friends who makes expensive dinner parties so she can live under the illusion that she is popular, liked, has a social life. No price is too big for this. She is someone who craves family. Who watches a lot of TV.

She knows Doreen, too, because she has known a lot of people just like Doreen.

Doreen is listening to whatever Elaine is saying. Or maybe she has bored herself to sleep. Denise imagines Julie buying lobster, stone crabs, shrimp, clams, whatever she can get that will impress. She cleans her whole house, chills expensive wine, or maybe even champagne. She takes a bath, puts on her make-up, sets her table, *waits for you, for your friends, the ones she's invited to welcome you to Miami Beach. When you get there, she'll serve drinks and hors d'oeuvres, the dreaded cheese, and then a full elaborate dinner to people who do not want to be there. She probably baked a key lime pie because we all do when people visit Miami Beach. And then laughing you all will leave and she'll be up for hours cleaning up from a dinner party no one wanted to come to. Her back will hurt and her legs will be tired and no one will even call the next day to say thanks.*

"Yeah, you could say something like that. You could tell her we have to leave at 8:00 because you made these other plans for us before you found out about the dinner. *You could invite her to go with you. She'd probably like that* She won't care about not being invited. No, she won't expect to be invited at all. She doesn't go out like that. And can you imagine taking her to Mansion or Set in one of those matching outfits? *I hope she poisons your fish* What? That's not my problem."

What IS your problem?

"She should have thought about that first before going out and buying all the stuff and doing all the work. *Thought about what? That she was making your life miserable by inviting you over for dinner?* Yeah, yeah, I know but you know what? I can't help that. I think it's a lot of nerve to just assume people want to do that, come over to your house and eat the food you decided to make *food you like, food she knows you like*…what? Ok, ok, so she's making fish for me but Jesus Christ, Elaine, does that mean I have to happy about it?"

Sort of. At least grateful. Or sensitive. It's a couple hours of your life.

"Ok, fine. That's a plan. I'll just have a drink up here first. I'll wait downstairs for you at 6:00. What kind of car do you have now. Oooo, black Beemer, how nice for you. Yeah, the flowered sundress. Ok? Ok, I gotta go. Crap, it's after 11:00 already!"

11:00? Already. Denise turns off her TV. She puts on shorts and a t-shirt and goes to the gym in the building. She gets on the stationary bike and pedals her heart out for an hour but no one who remotely resembles Doreen comes in.

She walks quickly out to the beach and heads toward Ocean Drive. 20 minutes one way and 20 minutes back but maybe Doreen changed her mind about working out all together or, if she is walking, maybe she is on the sand instead of the stone path that runs behind the building, where Denise is.

Or maybe on Lincoln Road. Denise walks quickly past her building and reaches Lincoln Road. It's hot and her legs ache from the biking but she walks the full 8 pedestrian blocks up Lincoln and the full 8 back down, the whole time looking at all the women who could be Doreen.

Upstairs, Denise showers, puts on the flowered sundress which, blessedly, fits and runs over to the spa at the Ritz. She sits in the pedicure chair, across from the manicure station, chooses a pale pink color for her toes, and waits. But the only people who come in are two teenagers and two blue-haired ladies. She has her eyebrows waxed after, in case Doreen is in the spa section, maybe laying in a white robe with cucumbers over her eyes waiting for her next service.

But she isn't. Maybe Denise got it wrong. Maybe Doreen was here at the spa first and now is lying in the sun or walking on the beach or riding the stationary bike. But it's too late to retrace now.

When Denise gets home, she looks great. Greater than she has looked in a long time. The walking has given her cheeks a good color, she has clean eyebrows and a great pedicure. She looks like she is ready for a party.

Denise tells herself that this is not at all crazy. It's more like fun. A fun thing to do. She is not going to Julie's party. At 5:45, she is downstairs in her car, waiting but just because she has to see Doreen. She listens to the radio, flips through a magazine, sips a Diet Coke she has brought with her. The valets smile and she waves. She mouths, "Waiting for someone." They nod their heads.

But by 6:30, no black BMWs have pulled into the circular drive, no women in flowered sundresses have stood outside waiting for a ride. So Denise drives away. If she knew where Julie lived, she'd drive by. She'd park in an inconspicuous place and watch all the people arrive. She'd know exactly who Doreen was when she saw her. She'd want to run her down. But she wouldn't, even though it would kill two birds with one stone because then Julie would be saved from having to throw this party. But Doreen never said Julie's address, not even her street, so Denise goes to get some gas and then, realizing she hasn't eaten all day and is hungry, to the McDonald's drive-thru. She orders a fish sandwich. She eats it on the way home, wondering what it is that people want from one another.

Saving Herself

What do people want from one another? Compassion? Company? Truth? People say they want the truth, that they value honesty above all else, but it isn't true. No one can tell the truth. No one can take it.

The morning after Julie's party, Doreen has resumed her place against Denise's door and is talking on her phone. Again. Denise cannot believe it.

"He's coming in on Delta...Friday, I don't know, around 9. That'll ruin my whole weekend for sure."

Denise storms to the door, puts her hand on the door knob. She is not going to put up with it this time. But then she stops because she hears,

"Yes, I know he's my father but for Christ's sake, he's 92 years old. He can't walk. He can't go anywhere. Why is he even coming here? What am I supposed to do? *Is this for real? Are you really saying this about your 92 year old father? Is no one safe from you?* No, I'm just tired, that's all. I'm tired, really tired . . . no, the party was the worst thing ever. Ok, fine, it wasn't the worst thing ever but it was pretty bad and . . . what? Why? Because no one wanted to be there and Julie made all this food and it was so hot in her house and . . . you know what?, You weren't even there so you don't really know *so it's not Elaine on the phone, because I'm sure Elaine went to Julie's party, and probably not Andrew either but now I wonder if it is Barb, since I don't know if Elaine invited her* no, it's just that Andrew was there OK,

I knew it wasn't Andrew and he brought his new girlfriend, and she was . . . fine, so she's not his new girlfriend but you know what I mean *what do you mean?* Why do you care about that? Ok, ok, she's around 30, I guess, with fake boobs and a short black bob hair cut. Yeah, yeah, just your type. Very funny *that is kind of funny but who are you talking to?* and anyway it was really embarrassing because Julie was like so annoying, running around her house, and it's so little, Jesus, so it felt like we were in this hot closet with her—she's gotten huge!!—touching people's clothes saying they're so cute and bringing them food and no one wanted it and saying to me, 'Doreen, have more lobster, I made it for you' and she brings it over and there was butter just dripping all off it and it was just about to get on my new dress and it was so disgusting and *oh my God what is the matter with you?*

Denise opens the bolt on her door. She thinks she is going to go out there and tell Doreen to go away but she is afraid. She hopes the sound of the bolt will be enough to send the message. But it has no effect on Doreen and then Denise knows she is trapped. She can't open the door, she can't pound on it to make Doreen stop and she can't walk away because if Denise didn't hear all this herself she would never believe in it. She has to stay.

". . . fine, you don't have to see me if you're fed up with me *what?* but I don't see why *I do* I didn't do anything to you. You don't even know my father so how can you say that? *I don't know your father and I think you are the most terrible person I've ever or never met.* Really? Well, you know what? In all three of my marriages *three marriages?* no one has been this insensitive to me, I'm just not used to it. *But you're used to doing it. How does it feel to be on the other end, you bitch* I find you very rude. It's like I'm watching my own movie and whatever happens, happens. Even when you were with me when we went to Segefredos . . . no, not that day, you were actually nice to me that day, but I'm talking about the day I got my hair done at Browne's and you were with your buddies . . . yeah, well, that's fine but you were such a total asshole to me and I just don't deserve to be treated like that . . ."

How do you deserve to be treated? Differently than how you treat other people? Why is that? Who the hell do you think you are?

Denise is surprised at the level of her fury. She doesn't know what to do with it. She has never had this depth of feeling for another person before. Even the people she has loved, like her family, or ones she's liked, even the people who have made her angry or hurt her feelings, she has never felt like this before.

"Well, if you would just listen to me" *it's impossible not to listen to you. Three marriages? Three men who want to be with you? How can that be? How could that ever be?*

And just like that, it becomes too much. Denise jiggles her door handle with all the power that is rushing through her and she knows Doreen can hear it because Denise can see the top of Doreen's head—blonde hair, streaked, spiky—moving through the peephole. But Doreen doesn't move. Denise re-bolts the lock and unbolts it again. As hard and loud as she can. She is trying to communicate something definitive.

". . . no, it's just that you wouldn't even say 'nice hair' or anything and you and your friends were talking about the stock market and you know I don't care about that or know anything about it and . . . what? Well, why did you invite me, then? *why would anyone invite you anywhere? I'm sure Julie's sorry she did* It's not the same thing. No, it's not. I didn't invite you to Julie's because I knew it would be boring for you but if I had . . . no, it had nothing to do with Andrew being there *it obviously had everything to do with Andrew being there* but I was saying that if I had invited you, then I would have just spent all my time making sure you were having a good time, not like what you did to me when I went to Segefredos."

Bullshit. You didn't invite this guy to Julie's because you were hoping the one thing you might have gotten out of it was a chance to. . .what? Get back at Andrew? Get back with Andrew? Be prettier than Andrew's not-so-new girlfriend? What do you look like? If this guy on the phone had gone to Julie's with you, you would have had to spend all your time there with him instead of flirting with Andrew. Who do you think you're fooling?

"You are just too rude to me. Fine, if you don't want to see me, see other people. It's fine. I don't care. I didn't come down here for you, anyway. I came down here to get tan, get some exercise, lose some weight. And Elaine and I have plans tonight anyway, so . . . why do you care about her? She's in the apartment sleeping. *Who is this person in the apartment always sleeping while you are talking on the phone practically in my apartment?* She's a big slug. Who cares? She has no idea . . . .why? Because it's a free apartment for God's sake, who wouldn't do it . . . She doesn't care. She has her own friend . . . No, she has no idea, I told you . . . so what? Who am I hurting? *Everyone. Anyone you know. Anyone near you.* Go go shopping with her, out to dinner sometimes before I go out at night. I buy her groceries sometimes . . . what are you talking about? She didn't even want to go to Julie's, she hates Julie, and besides she's a pain to be with, you know it, she . . . oh really? You are such an asshole. You're nicer to her than you are to me. So what? So what if she fixed us up? No big favor really, not the way things are now. Right? . . . Helllooo? I said, right? I told you, she's sleeping in the apartment, I'm in the hallway. She can't hear me."

But I can. And I hate you. It's more than just Doreen's personality. It's the way she thinks she's better than everyone else. The superiority. It's the rudeness, the inconsideration. That it's ok for Doreen to be doing this, to be leaning on Denise's door talking in a full voice, again, with no idea that there is someone in that apartment so deeply disturbed. It's the not caring.

Denise goes and gets her garbage, ties it up, and returns to the door. She has had it. She is just about to open the door when,

"Hon? Mean? You think I'm being mean? How can you say I'm being mean? You're the one who's being mean, to me. You are so rude to me and I don't understand why because I tried with you. I did. And you just . . . no, really, none of my husbands ever acted like that, not even Andrew and he . . . what? Oh, that's nice. Real nice . . . so maybe you're right, ok? Maybe his new girlfriend with the fake boobs is nicer than me, so what? That doesn't give you the right to *what gives you the right? What gives you the right to be here in my life?* I don't know. I don't know what to tell you now. If you don't want to see me, it's fine. But do you mean just tonight or never again at all . . . well, you'd better know. You'd better figure it out because I'm not going to go through this again, I can tell you that . . . I don't know. I don't know if I want to see you anymore, how can I know that when you act like this with me? You know, if you really loved me, you would . . ."

And then Denise cannot hear Doreen anymore. She has moved away. Denise looks out the peep hole and can't see Doreen. She can only hear remnants of her voice fading in the hall.

". . . uh huh . . . yes . . . I do, I . . . hon, come on . . ."

When it's gone, inexplicably Denise feels like crying. She wants to feel relieved. She doesn't feel sorry for the guy on the other end of the phone. She's sure Julie has recovered by now. She knows it only takes a day or two to get over a dinner party no one really wanted to go to, to eat up all the leftovers, put the good platters and wine glasses away. And then Denise is crying and it makes her even more angry than she was before. She pounds on her own door now, pounds until her hand hurts. She is still holding her tied-up garbage bag and full on crying. She hates Doreen more than she has ever hated anything before and without knowing she's going to do it, she opens her door fast, yanks up the garbage and rushes out of her apartment.

Doreen is at the far end of the hall. So far away, she looks tiny but Denise can see that she is tiny. At first, Denise thinks Doreen is wearing yet another sundress but then she thinks, no, it's a towel. A towel. In the hallway of the fifth floor of the apartment building. Denise wants to set her on fire.

But then, as if she has been caught leering, Denise rushes across the hall to the trash room, throws her garbage down the chute, and stops. She breathes, wipes her eyes, and breathes again but the tears keep coming. She wants to go back into her apartment but now she is afraid Doreen might be making her way back down the hall and Denise doesn't know what she will say to her if she opens the door and Doreen is standing there. She does not have any experience to draw on.

Denise puts her ear to the door and hears nothing. The coast seems clear. She gathers herself together and steps back out into the hallway.

And there she is. Leaning against Denise's door, listening intently to the guy on the other end of the phone and nodding her head. She is definitely wearing a towel. Her feet are bare and her hair is wet. She is older than Denise thought, probably in her 40s. Old enough to have three marriages. Old enough to know better. She is too tan and her toes are painted red. Denise thinks Doreen is pretty, probably prettier with makeup.

". . . I know . . . me, too . . . ok. I'm so sorry, hon. Yes, I want to. I do. I want to . . ."

"What do you want?" Denise says out loud. There cannot be more than four feet between them. "What on earth do you want?"

"What should I wear?" Doreen asks. "Well of course I care what you think, why wouldn't I? If I didn't care, I wouldn't ask, would I? Jeez, why do you always have to be like this?"

"Because you are like this," Denise says. *Why are you like this? How can anyone be like this?*

Denise is leaning against the trash room door and Doreen is leaning against Denise's door. It could be a stand-off. Doreen doesn't hear Denise or notice her and although Denise knows what she wants to do—pull Doreen's towel off, yank out some of her wet hair, stomp on her red toes until they bleed—she just stands there. She can't help herself. She is still crying. She wants to go home.

Then Doreen looks up, straight at Denise. She says, "Hon, what's wrong? Are you ok?" They are looking right at each other.

"I gotta go," Doreen says into the phone. "I'll call you later, I love you, Yes, hon, I do. I love you but I have to go now" and then,

"Hon?" Doreen steps toward Denise, puts her free hand out. "Hon? Are you ok? What's wrong?"

But Denise doesn't hear her.

The Secret World of Women

Abbey is having a party tonight.

Sloane is tired, already a little drunk, and does not really want to go but only for those two reasons. Oh, and this one—her hair: it is dirty and too gray and smells like smoke. She should have gone to the salon weeks ago to have the gray roots dyed out but because she is always railing against female vanity, she didn't. And she should have quit smoking years ago, but that's another story.

It's 6:30 pm and the party starts at 7:30. She has already made little tortilla spirals filled with cream cheese, scallions and Tabasco. She made her own salsa, too. If she could have roused herself to go shopping, she would have dished up something much more spectacular but the prospect of aisles and choices and the pressure to be observant was exhausting: Sloane is an English professor who writes poems about women in grocery stores. So she had opened a bottle of wine instead, rifled around the cupboards and refrigerator and, *olé*, tortillas and salsa.

She has to leave at 7:15, so she pours one more glass of wine, which she does not need and that could severely impair her driving, and realizing that showering is out of the question (too much work), thinks about how she will have to put on scented deodorant if she really plans to leave the house and stand next to other people at Abbey's party.

Abbey is married to Ben. They are wonderful and Sloane loves them. They are having a party for friends of theirs—Gavin and Daniella—who have just gotten married. Everyone loves Gavin and no one loves Daniella, except Gavin; the wedding was an impromptu affair that took place in a notary's driveway (his house was under renovation), and was basically a joyless occasion so Abbey and Ben decided to spruce it up with a post-vows party. Abbey will have fun whether Sloane shows up or not, but she sounded like she really wanted Sloane to come. Beside, Sloane made food—which she'd just end up throwing away because no one eats appetizers they make for a party they don't go to—and bought Gavin and Daniella two cheap wine glasses from Pier One and a miniature bottle of Chianti. Get up, Sloane says to herself: get up and get dressed and go to the party!

In her closet are a lot of clothes that would look much better on her if she lost ten pounds. As it is, her no longer extant waist hangs over the sides of all her pants unless she continually sucks her stomach in, which takes work. And hurts. At a loss for choice and time, she pulls on hip-hugger black levis and a black t-shirt with a green square in the middle. She bought this top at a trendy store on Collins Ave. so at least she will appear hip; it has a thin strip of green on the back, below the collar. Very hip. There is a lot of pressure to appear hip when you are shaped by the name Sloane; people expect you to be beyond the ordinary, to possess some secret knowledge because no one else has your name. Years ago, in college, Sloane stopped explaining that her mother named her after the nurse who played Jeopardy! and Wheel of Fortune with her during labor and whose first name she never knew. It turned out to be easier and less time-consuming to just pretend to be cool.

Sloane pulls her too long, very curly, dirty hair that needs to be colored up into a clip, sprays on some perfume, grabs the gift and the tortillas and goes.

Very carefully, she drives to Abbey and Ben's since she has already had wine. In a shorter time than she would have liked, she pulls into their driveway. She leans over to the passenger seat to get the food (the gift is already in a bag over her wrist), and uses her free hand to check her hair when, supernaturally, the hair clip snaps apart and the unruly smelly hair falls down over Sloane's shoulders.

Hmmm.

Abbey is, as predicted, very happy to see her. She is an adorable girl, as are her friends, Caroline and Helene—all three greet Sloane warmly and she is grateful for them. She is also aware that she must smell like a dead animal who rolled in air freshener and that she is in dire need of a hair implement. Quickly, Abbey, Caroline, Helene and Sloane scurry into Abbey's bedroom. Sloane loves having girlfriends. Abbey gives her a little hair clip; she pulls only part of her hair up and begins to wrestle the clip into place when it comes apart in her hands.

"Sorry, Abs," Sloane says, and everyone laughs, looking at each other and then at themselves in the big dresser mirror. Abbey, Caroline and Helene are 30, 31, and 32, respectively, and each one is a beautiful, fashionable girl. Great hair, good teeth, clear skin. Sloane is 44 and in the mirror sees her permanent laugh lines, which come from sorrow, and theirs (which only appear when they laugh) that come from the mirth of youth. She also sees three angry red pimples on her chin that could masquerade as boils and laments the fact that middle age has taken away everything from her youth except acne. Abbey gives her another clip, a bigger one, and very carefully Sloane subdues her hair, despite the fact that her reflection proves she has transformed into one of the witches from *Macbeth*. Enough of this mirror.

Where is the beer?

Ben brings Sloane a beer. She pecks his cheek in thanks. Then she turns and kisses Gavin and congratulates him. He looks sad. Once, some months ago, she made out with him in a bar; the next day, he claimed not to remember. They get on fine now but when she sees his sad married eyes she thinks, "screw you, asshole" and gulps some beer. Then she turns to give a congratulatory kiss to Daniella, who has taken a liking to Sloane (she either does or does not know about the making out but since everyone hates her, Sloane is her "go to" girl). Daniella takes Sloane's hand and pulls her outside to her car, where she has a picture of the driveway wedding she wants to show Sloane. Sloane goes without asking why Daniella doesn't just bring the picture in and show everyone: the beer is cold; Sloane is tired; it's more polite to smoke outside.

This event takes very little time and before the cigarette is finished, Sloane and Daniella are making their way back to the house. Two more guests are arriving: one is a huge guy who likes his muscles, wearing a black t-shirt with the sleeves rolled up and very tight black pants. Not Sloane's type, she thinks, which is a good thing since behind him is an extraordinarily gorgeous girl— tall, thin and curvy, wearing a tiny white t-shirt that rises above her flat tan belly, gray hip-hugger pants which actually hug her hips—as opposed to Sloane's which delineate her extra ten pounds—and running shoes. She has short cropped blonde hair and the kind of perfect face you wouldn't think was real unless you looked at it yourself, as Sloane is doing now. So she lights another cigarette once inside (because other people are smoking in here, too) and thinks —so you're a runner? Big deal. Fuck you. Sloane has some anger issues.

The blonde girl is Alex, the black-clad muscle guy's wife, and she goes to the kitchen and immediately begins slicing a whole smoked salmon she has brought. She is chopping at it, actually, and even though Sloane knows how to separate the pieces so they don't come out looking like raw hacked human flesh, she says nothing. She doesn't want to stand next to this girl who, she hates to admit, seems very nice, so she walks through the house and goes out to the back patio.

Caroline and Helene are out there and Sloane is grateful. She sits down in a chair and joins into their conversation. Actually, she is more listening than joining, a trait she has cultivated in response to a general lack of anything much to say at parties. Besides, all the girls at the table are talking about people Sloane doesn't know.

It does not take long before Sloane realizes that the combination of fatigue, alcohol and a story about someone's mother's trip to Indianapolis has created a pall of boredom threatening suffocation; and she's only been here for fifteen minutes. Lamenting her choice to come at all, she begins to look around to see what else is going on. Through the porch door, she sees into the kitchen and notices two guys staring quizzically at her tortillas. One is coiffed: hair slicked back, little foo-manchu goatee, nicely pressed shirt tucked into jeans. Behind him is a short guy with a funny fisherman's type hat, odd pants that only come to his mid-calf but seemingly on purpose, and a plaid shirt. He reminds Sloane for some reason of Bruce Springsteen, who for a long time was the only person she would have ever even considered marrying. It has oc-curred to her more recently that the limitations that consideration produced might have something to do with the fact that she is still single.

Lately, the lack of romance in Sloane's life has become a point of conten-tion between her enlightened self and her darker, more critical doppelganger: Women need men like fish need bicycles, she chants during these arguments, revealing her age and lack of a solid position; get a life, the doppelganger re-plies, or at least a bike: maybe you'll meet someone on the road.

For a long time she had done neither, relying on her need to work—to write more poems—in order to get promoted. It was a legitimate excuse for not wanting to face what she would have to do now, at 44, in order to get back in the game. But here is a guy she is looking at who might do; in addition to looking like The Boss, he is dressed as though he doesn't care how he looks. My kind of guy, Sloane thinks, and finishes her whole beer in three swallows. Now, beneath the heavy buzz, she has discovered a purpose: she is going to fall in love.

But it's the coiffed guy who comes out and takes the seat next to her. His name is John. He is 35, recently separated from his wife, more drunk than Sloane is, and chatty. It's good—he is a nice guy and Sloane is a good listener. Then he asks Sloane what she does and she tells him she's an English teacher. Big mistake. Suddenly, he feels compelled to recount all of the Shakespeare plays his father took him to when he was a boy and then begins to ask literary questions: if this had been *Who Wants To Be A Millionaire?* Sloane might be living in Aruba now.

"OK," he says, "who wrote the . . . the . . . The Talking Heart?"

"You mean "The Tell-Tale Heart," she asks, guessing.

"Yeah."

"Poe."

"Who?"

"Poe. Edgar Allen Poe."

"Right," he says, "OK. Who said something about something bad in England?"

"In Denmark?" Sloane says, crediting years of teaching for having figured this one out so quickly.

"Huh?"

"There's something rotten in the state of Denmark?" she says.

"Right," he says, "Hamlet says it." Sloane is about to say that although the line is from *Hamlet*, the prince doesn't say it but decides to lament her empty cup instead.

"I'll get you a beer," he says.

"Good," she says, "I'll wait here," because despite these dumb questions, he is sweet and she has nowhere else to go.

When he returns and stops quizzing her, the conversation improves. He is actually a nice guy, smart and talkative, and Sloane finds that she is having a fine time. Still, she keeps looking around for the Bruce Springsteen look-alike. When she cannot find him, she finds instead some words forming inside her mouth and lets them out: "So what do you do?"

John works for his brother in the family business: they own a junkyard. John seems to like his brother, who is five years older than John—making him around 40—but he is clearly not happy with the way his brother bosses him around.

"Like the other day," he begins to explain, "I got to work early, turned the air-conditioning on, got the invoices ready and then he comes in and starts yelling at me about . . ." but then John stops his story very abruptly. Sloane looks up to where John is looking and sees that he has been interrupted by the appearance of the Bruce Springsteen guy, the guy in the funny hat. He looks at Sloane, Sloane looks at him, and he sits down in the vacant chair that is across from them.

"I'll finish this later," John whispers, and then in a regular loud voice he says to Sloane, "This is my brother, Billy." When he turns to introduce Sloane, his phone falls off the clip he has attached to his waist. "Damn phone," John says, standing up, "it's always falling off this thing." He replaces it and sits down again. "Anyway, yeah," he says, "this is my brother, Billy."

Sloane is already in love with the brother Billy because he is short and messy and looks like The Boss. But when she gets to know him a little better, her blind devotion seems more legitimate. He is quiet, unassuming, funny and beneath that hat, very handsome. He talks a bit about the plays he saw with his brother since John introduced Sloane as an English teacher but then they talk about other things, too. They talk about other books, about Miami, about politics. Then they talk about music and Sloane waits for him to burst into a chorus of "Born to Run," which she normally is in situations like this; instead, however, she gently tries to maneuver the remaining strands of red-colored hair over the gray, hoping she does not disrupt Abbey's hairclip.

They sit there for a long time. Ultimately, Sloane realizes she could sit there all night, except that she knows she cannot have any more beer and Billy has begun the shifting and crowd-scanning that signals departure. Sensitive to innuendo, especially when her own future is at stake, she immediately says, "I have to go soon." He echoes, "I have to go soon too" but neither of them budges. This seems to Sloane a sign of something, but she is too drunk to figure out what. Just then, Abbey appears, bright and beautiful, and sits down with Sloane and the brothers. Another woman who looks very cultured and well-traveled—she is wearing a most hip small black dress, funky eye-glasses and had the guts to toss a feather boa around her shoulder—is sitting across from Abbey. Sloane wonders what this hip woman is named and is not surprised to find out that she is called Sonora when Abbey introduces everyone. "Sonora is a writer," Abbey says, "and Sloane is a writer, too. A published one."

The woman nods in approval but Billy asks, "What do you write?"

"Poems," Sloane says.

"Oh yeah?" he says. "Send me some," and he pulls out a business card to hand to her.

"Do you have email?" she asks, happy and nervous at the same time because she knows that if she owned any of her own business cards, she would never give them to anyone unless she really wanted that person to get in touch with her. Sloane tends to second guess people based upon what she would do in similar situations. She ought to consider outgrowing this.

"Yeah, but people have a hard time getting through to me on email for some reason," Billy says. This does not seem like the innuendo she would normally take it to be, though it should have; instead, she asks him to recite his email address (which does not appear on the card) and he does: she commits it to memory and is already thinking about which poems she will send him. One long one? Two shorter ones? And ode to him that she might write tonight?

During all this time, John has brought Sloane another beer, which she has decided not to drink, since she has to drive home and is determined not to forget Billy's email address.

Eventually the reality of her condition combines with a vague memory that she ought to be the least bit mysterious and unavailable so she says, "I have to go," and stands up; then her heart does a little flip because Billy stands up and says, "Me, too." Sloane wonders what will happen when they walk out together, an exit she plans on maneuvering, when John says to her, "Can I get a ride home?"

John lives on the beach. Sloane lives on the beach. The beach is south and Billy lives much further north than they are now, so Sloane tells John that she'd be happy to drive him home: the ease with which she says this she is sure is not lost on Billy—she is a kind, caring person who is happy to do things for others.

They all go inside to make their goodbyes—Gavin, Daniella, and Ben are standing in the corner; three girls who must have gone to the same hairdresser and the same dress shop are sitting on the couch; Abbey, Caroline and Helene have followed Sloane and the brothers inside. There is a whirl of hugs and kisses and thank you's and goodbyes and then Sloane is certain she is walking out to her car with John and Billy but when she gets to her car for what she has imagined would be a most meaningful moment, a movie movement, she realizes Billy is already gone.

OK, she says in her fuzzy head, *OK. Fine. At least I didn't say anything stupid.* And then she is proud of herself. Still, during the entire ride to the beach, she resists the urge to tell John that she is in love with his brother. Instead, she listens to John's sad story of why he is separated from his wife and finds that she truly finds it sad (especially since she is so far gone by now that she believes herself to be on the cusp of a great love affair and so can be particularly sympathetic to the less fortunate). Suddenly Sloane, who spends more time talking to her selves and the women who populate her poems than to real live people, is a professional psychologist: she encourages John to call his wife, apologize, be contrite, start again; when she drops him off in front of the cheap motel he's been relegated to since his wife dumped him, one that doesn't even have a phone, she says, "Call her on your cell phone the moment you get in." He assures Sloane he will, thanks her for the great advice, gives her a brotherly kiss on the cheek, and goes inside.

All in a night's work, Sloane says to herself, satisfied with her new-found skills in psychotherapy.

Emphasis on psycho, the doppelganger says, but Sloane ignores her and races home.

Immediately, she turns on her computer and writes this email:
Billy:
Just dropped your brother off safely and wanted to email you before I forgot your address. If you get this, let me know and I'll send some poems.
It was really nice to meet you. Sloane

She hits Send. Then she spends several minutes wondering if she should have written "Dear Billy' instead of just "Billy," or if she should have sent one of her best poems so he could not help falling in love with her; then she reasons that maybe her poems will make him hate her because they are sad and complicated and maybe not all that good. She feels the familiar pangs of working herself up into a frenzy over a situation that hasn't even taken place yet, and also the familiar pains of being too tired to fight with her selves any longer so she goes into the bathroom to wash her face. Careful not to greet her reflection in the mirror, lest she be forced to narrow the gap between who she is and what she is behaving like, she flops into bed and falls asleep dreaming of Billy letting her wear his hat.

Sloane wakes up at five in the morning with a wicked headache and tries to feel her way in the dark to the computer: She foregoes coffee to turn on email: this should have been a red flag. There is a message from someone she doesn't know offering ways to reach financial freedom in 3 days, an advertisement for Viagra—a product she hopes she has a chance to discover is not needed—and a message from her friend who is in South Africa and who writes in what is the middle of Sloane's night but her morning. She is ashamed that she had convinced herself Billy would get up this early to see if she had emailed him (it occurs to her that she should try her hand at writing fiction, as she is so good at living it), so she deletes the finance guy, answers Laura, and goes to make coffee. Then she reads the paper. Then she turns on her computer again but this time, writes the first few lines of what could become a short story.

Then the phone rings. It is Abbey. She tells Sloane that John has called her to say he left his phone in Sloane's car—apparently it came off of its clip again—and she tells Sloane that she is supposed to call Billy to make arrangements to return it.

"Billy?" Sloane says. "Are you sure?"

"That's what John said. He left Billy's number and you're supposed to call him."

OK. OK.

Sloane swigs some cold coffee, wishing she had some scotch to put in it. She wonders why, if John could find a phone, he didn't ask Abbey for Sloane's number and just call her himself; after all, the motel he lives in is just up the street. But then she steadies herself into the reality that, despite all her fantasies, she didn't really believe: Billy likes her. He wants to see her. This is a match that was meant to be.

She brushes her teeth and her hair as if she is going to meet Billy instead of going to call him, and then she goes for the phone. She dials the number and a deep male voice answers.

"Billy?" she says.

"Yeah." He says this through a yawn.

"It's Sloane."

There is silence at the other end of the phone. He doesn't remember her. He has no idea who she is or why she is calling. Sloane moves the receiver from her face and heads it back down to its cradle when her doppelganger takes over and practically smashes the phone into Sloane's chin.

"From Abbey's party last night? Your brother left his phone in my car?"

She says everything as if it is a question, as if she is asking if this is what she is supposed to say.

"Yeah," he says, "oh yeah" and then sounds downright cheery. He proceeds to tell Sloane how John called him early in the morning about the phone, how he was panicked, is always losing his phone, etc.

"Listen," he says, "we're going to breakfast up the street from where you live. Do you want to come with us?"

"Sure," Sloane says, before she really knows if she wants to do this or not; frankly, in the realm of romance, Sloane operates much more effectively when it is only taking place in her head. It's one thing to fall in love and fantasize the bliss of it all; it's quite another thing to face the object of your affection in the bright Miami sunshine over a bowl of oatmeal. But Sloane's other half is poised and ready: she knocks Sloane out cold and agrees to meet Billy and John for breakfast at 11:00.

And it is now 10:15. She takes a fast shower and tries to decide what to wear. How should she look? Sleepy and sexy? Well, that might be a good choice except Sloane does not know how to create that look. Teacher-like? On a Sunday morning? Absolutely not. Healthy? Yeah, healthy and active and just in for a quick coffee before her busy sporty day. So she puts her bathing suit on, since swimming is the only kind of exercise she can stand, and then is about to grab her keys and go when a quick movement past the big mirror in the hall reveals she has not put anything on over the bathing suit.

Sloane sits down on the kitchen floor and shakes her head, which clearly is still laboring under last night's bacchanalia or she would have clothes on. She bends her legs, tucks her knees under her chin, and begins to cry. What is she doing? He's just a guy. Is she that far gone that a mundane conversation that she can barely remember has become the precipice on which her life precariously teeters?

Stop being so dramatic, the doppelganger says, and go put some clothes on before you're late.

Sloane gets up and tries on three outfits before choosing her old faded jeans and a black t-shirt, a settling back into her most comfortable self. It's Sunday morning on the beach, she reasons (though knows she wears this old standby every opportunity she gets). She thinks about driving or walking but then chooses driving because (a) she doesn't want to be sweaty when she gets there and, (b) the phone is in her car so she has to get the car anyway.

She arrives at 11:15 and, looking inside, sees they are not there yet. She stands outside the restaurant for 20 minutes before they arrive. When they walk up, she is nonchalantly flipping through the *New Times*; what they don't know, however, is that she can't read a word without her glasses, which she did not bring. That comfortable, she was not.

She gives John the phone and he says jokingly, "You didn't even charge it," to which she responds, "I wouldn't know how. I think I'm the only person in Miami without a cell phone." She thinks this makes her sound as down-to-earth and unpretentious as she thinks Billy is, so she is pleased.

They go in. They sit down, Sloane next to John and Billy across from them, just like last night: Sloane takes this as a sign. For some reason (which Sloane hopes has something to do with her), Billy has brought a book. He sets it on the table, so Sloane picks it up and pretends to peruse it; since she doesn't have her glasses, she can only see the title but the gods are with her because seeing the title, she realizes she has already seen the movie and can talk semi-intelligently about this work. Luck is even more on her side: Billy has not read the book yet and didn't even know the movie was out, so she is saved from making a fool of herself. Phew.

Then Billy mentions mountain biking; Sloane forces the fish on bicycles thing right out of her head and asks where the best places are to ride in Miami: this quick save gives them something else to chat about and Sloane is relieved. But the sad truth is Sloane is not a good chatter: she is a good friend, a good intellectual partner, and a person who can make witty banter with the best of them; she is a person who can whip together a Mexican delight from odds and ends in her cupboards. But she is not a good small-talker and already she is feeling as though Billy is on to her. Then out of nowhere he states that he is re-reading *The Autobiography of Ben Franklin* which, despite Sloane's vast education in English and American literature, she has not read; she wants to disappear under the table, wondering why the gods could not have made him mention one of the umpteen million books she has read. He probably thinks I'm an imposter, she frets, a fraud. To confirm her suspicions, then, he says,

"So you're a teacher. What do you have to have for that? Certification?"

Sloane is a professor but she calls herself a teacher because professors teach and because she never wants to appear to be a snob but now she does the unthinkable for any self-respecting feminist, which up until this moment she had thought she was. She says,

"Well, where I teach, you don't need to be certified. In fact, I couldn't teach in public school even if I wanted to because I'm not certified. But . . ." and here, inexcusably, she puts her eyes down into her lap and says, "I have a Ph.D." The doppelganger applauds her feigned shame but she is preparing for her own execution.

And thunder and lightening are bolting through her heart, which she deserves since the amount of time and effort and stamina it took to get that Ph.D. should make her nothing but proud, but here she is behaving as if it is embarrassing to be so degreed. Let's face it: cute boys who run junkyards don't like old women with Ph.D.'s.

But when she picks her head up and sees that he is smiling at her, she wants to jump across the table and yell, "Where have you been all my life?" Thankfully, she doesn't; instead, she puts some butter on her toast, takes a bite and sips her American coffee. Sloane relaxes into this familiar activity, the eating of breakfast, and happily turns her attention to John, who has begun talking about last night's party. He is trying to remember all the people who were there and he starts with Abbey's best friends. Billy is trying to place Caroline and Helene—trying to figure out who is who—and Sloane smiles, secretly thinking he's doing that for her benefit: all other girls blend into one another when he's sitting across from Sloane. So she takes advantage of her inflated position in the world of women and describes each girl.

"But who was the blonde?" Billy says, neither of whom is Caroline or Helene, so Sloane thinks of Laura, the fourth of the Abbey-Caroline-Helene consortium. But Laura was out of town this weekend and so was not at the party. Still, Sloane says, "Laura?"

"No," he says, "blonde. Tall."

But that is Laura and surely they have met before so Sloane says "Laura" again because, basically, she is back to where she usually resides: in the place where she has no idea what else to say. Doppel is slowly winding a noose around her neck.

But then he says, "I don't think so: this was the tall blonde girl in grey pants."

Oh, God.

Alex.

Alex of the smoked salmon, the amazing body, the extraordinary face, the husband (though what does it matter now?) with the black muscle t-shirt. And then the walls of this little Cuban restaurant quickly begin to close in because the Billy who wears funny hats and looked like he shared Sloane's lack of concern over appearance, who drove all the way to the beach for breakfast when Sloane could have walked up the street to return John's phone, who brings a book to breakfast and gives her his card and asks for her poems is actually a guy who remembered what a beautiful girl he didn't even meet was wearing. And it's not like she was wearing a slinky dress or a thong; it's not like she was one of the three girls on the couch with identically frizzy hair and fake breasts who John called The Witches of Eastwick: she was wearing plain gray pants. And Billy remembered them.

Sloane looks at her watch as if she is late and she is—she is too late, as usual, and so she says "I have to go." Well, this is the truth: now there is no doubt that she has to go. Like items on a conveyer belt, everything that has happened within the last 15 hours passes through her mind, passing her right by although she is standing there trying to grab at least one of them before they disappear. Each item that had been so invested with meaning now meant nothing at all.

"Stay where you are," demands her other self. "What's the big deal? So she had a great butt in grey pants and you had one straining to get out of your pants? So what?"

Now Sloane is actually laughing out loud, hoping they are all still a bit drunk so no one will be able to fully remember this scene. She stands up too fast and knocks what remains of her American coffee out of its cup. She opens her mouth to say "Nice to meet you" and instead a hiccup escapes. She looks around the table for her sunglasses until she remembers that they are on top of her head.

"Where are you going?" Billy asks.

"Oh, me?" she says, thinking she is going to buy a mountain bike so she can ride off a cliff. "I'm going swimming," she comes up with and, because apparently she has not humiliated herself enough, she lifts up her black t-shirt to show the red tank suit.

Something is seriously wrong with me, she thinks, as if she has just discovered this; and then, to prove it, she moves her hands behind her back to push away the chair she has already pushed away. "Bye," she says, trying to sound bright and carefree, and then tears toward the door of the Puerto Saga Restaurant, ungracefully dodging other tables, people waiting for tables, a big metal box housing newspapers. She hurls herself out the door and thinks now would be the perfect time to hurl all of her various selves under some unsuspecting tourist's car.

The Other Mothers

I know they call me "The Captain's Wife" because they don't remember my name. Or they don't know it. Or they do and don't care. They see me every day at school, when all the mothers and their children and the teachers gather around the Headmistress for Morning Announcements. Sometimes the other mothers say "Hi" or "Hola" when I approach them, but then they turn back to each other. Into each other. I can't tell them apart. They are impossibly thin, polished and flawless like statues. Each one is astonishingly beautiful in different ways yet interchangeable: at one time or another, each one has touched me on the shoulder to compensate for her disinterest.

When Mrs. Bascomb, the Headmistress, claps her hands, signifying that she is about to speak, everyone goes quiet. But this morning, I cannot stop the screaming in my head. I am looking up, squinting, concentrating as hard as I can even though it is impossible to see inside the cockpit of the plane that is flying through the sky. My husband, The Captain, is a pilot. I think he is having an affair.

I have three small daughters and when they see me looking up they look up too, see the plane, and begin waving wildly and screaming, "it's Daddy, hi Daddy, hi Daddy" as the plane flies by. Four-year-old Scarlett is in my arms, shrieking. I know this will get me in trouble with the Headmistress but I do not like to reprimand my kids for being kids. Still, I put a finger to her lips.

Mrs. Bascomb is frowning. She has a small pointy face with a long nose and it is clear she struggles to find herself attractive. When she is displeased, as she is now, all of her features press in toward that nose until she looks like a snarling rodent. She shouts out my children's names—*Alexandra, Sabrina, Scarlett* —in her stern voice but either they don't hear or don't care.

"Mrs. Palmer," she says to me, "We need to return to the morning announcements, don't we?" It is, obviously, a rhetorical question. "Isn't that right, Palmer Girls?" I want to pull my hair out of my head because the other mothers are staring at me. I bite the inside of my cheeks instead.

Can't you keep your children quiet? I imagine her wanting to say to me. All of the other children are standing up straight in their uniforms, even the four year olds, and my knees start to shake. I am helpless. On this private residential island where we live now, it seems I can never do anything right. I feel the other mothers' impatience.

But then the plane is gone and the girls quiet down as if nothing has happened, and the Headmistress continues on. Her voice is too bright, overly enthusiastic, and I know it is because I and my children have disrupted this daily droning on of what is to happen today at The Island Preparatory School. Mrs. Bascomb seems oblivious to what I am sure is this community's resigned tolerance of her. Like me, Mrs. Bascomb is an outsider, new to the Island School; unlike me, or so it seems, Mrs. Bascomb is due a certain amount of feigned affection and respect.

I was pretty in college. I looked like all my girlfriends—country plump, fresh-faced, dull straight hair cut blunt with bangs. What made me stand out were my freckles. I have freckles everywhere, up and down my arms, all over my chest, covering the bridge of my nose. The other mothers have the smoothest skin I have ever seen, like cream or coffee or cocoa, depending where they're from. You want to drink them. Even the ones who are obviously over 40. Not a single spot or blemish. I know it's rude but I can't help staring at their skin.

When the Morning Announcements are over, I want to kiss my ten-year-old Alexandra good bye but Ali—as her friends here have taken to calling her—is already moving away in the pack of fifth graders. I pat eight-year-old Sabrina on the head as she heads to her classroom. The other mothers have disbanded and are walking their children to class. I will take Scarlett to the Pre-School room.

I imagine the other mothers, these beautiful women I have to stand next to every morning, whispering to each other, *what is she doing here?* I don't belong. I can't fit in. I am not gorgeous and glossy, enhanced and trim and tanned, but I know I am nice, fun to be with, and I want to show my best self. Because for now, for at least the next year, I am here.

Since we arrived, a month ago, I have tried different ways of making friends but I always get it wrong. It's hard. Sometimes I can't talk at all because everyone is speaking a language I don't understand. Mostly it's Spanish and either they assume I know Spanish or they know I don't. Other times, I talk too much, I talk without thinking and I hear words coming out of my own mouth that I don't remember ever being in my head. I say hello too fast and with too many words—*Hey, hi there, hello, que pasa, what's up, hola!*—ask too many questions, forget to take a breath. Everyone is foreign, almost no one is American, all the accents are always rushing past me. Once, Erika Fernandez, who is lively and stunning and Cuban, was telling me something. She was speaking English but her accent was heavy and I didn't know what she was saying but I was afraid because none of the mothers had ever told me anything before and I was concentrating on her words and suddenly I said, *Aiyii, Mami* because I heard Erika herself say that to another mother once but as soon as it came out, in my Midwestern twang, I knew how stupid it sounded and I couldn't get it back. The world seemed to freeze up and all its air disappeared. Erika raised her shoulders, cocked her head slightly, and walked away. I punched my forehead. Three times. But no one was looking at me.

When the airline transferred Roger from Cleveland to Miami, he made arrangements with a colleague who lived on The Island but was being transferred to Bogota to rent his house here for one year. We are not rich but suddenly we are living the same life as the wealthiest people in America. When we first arrived, I was overwhelmed with The Island's beauty, its privacy, the fact that you could only get there on a ferry. And if you were not a resident or a worker or your name was not on the Ferry Master's list, you were not getting there at all. Twice I have been mistaken for an uninvited guest. Four times for a worker. Roger says I can buy new clothes but I don't think that's the problem.

Roger has a completely different experience. He is thrilled to be living on The Island. When he goes to school functions, he walks right up to the parents and just starts talking. They all seem to love him. Maybe it's because he always wears his pilot's uniform. They engage him in conversations, invite him to golf or poker, want him to join them for Mojitos at the Island Club Bar. He goes.

I stay home. I cook and clean and raise my children. I am a good mother. When the girls are at school, I lay on the couch reading cookbooks or thinking up projects for my girls to do when they get home. Alexandra is already outgrowing me but sometimes I can lure her back in with a sewing project, if I have picked out a pattern she likes. The little ones still love fingerpaint, Play-dough, baking cookies, being read to. Sometimes I watch afternoon TV, soap operas, what my mother used to call the stories. The women on those shows could live here on this island. I think the other mothers make fun of my clothes. I do not look interesting, like anyone they think they should know. I think Roger is having an affair with Junior Captain Eleanor Buchanan.

But I know that was not him up in the sky this morning because when I get back from taking the girls to school, I hear the water running in the shower and know Roger is home. He has been flying for several days. As quickly as I can, I check his dirty clothes for lipstick or the scent of perfume but Ellie B, as she is called, is too smart to leave any trace of herself behind.

Before we came to The Island, we had what I think was a good marriage. We were happy. We laughed a lot. We had a lot of friends, they all had kids, we had barbeques, played charades, took all of our kids to the petting zoo or to ride the roller coasters at Geauga Lake. We hardly ever got mad at each other so we rarely had any big heavy discussions but when we needed to, we could.

I know when you move you can lose things but I didn't think you could lose something as big as that so when Roger gets out of the shower, I ask him about Ellie B. I have to. Otherwise, I can never stop looking.

"What are you talking about?" Roger says.

"I can tell," I say, "You talk about her all the time, you're with her more than you're here, you hardly pay any attention to me anymore."

"You're whining, Mallory," Roger responds, and not kindly. "And I'm exhausted. Cut it out already, will you?"

"I'm not whining," I say, remembering the times when if Roger thought I was upset, he would sit us down together, put his arm around me, tell me I was being foolish. I would be happy now to be foolish. But he does not comfort me so I say, "You're not happy."

"What are you talking about?" he says. "I'm perfectly happy."

"But I mean happy here, with us, at home."

"Of course I am. This is my home. You're my family. What could make me happier?"

"You don't seem like it," I say but I'm not explaining myself the way I want to. I am losing myself in the words that are not the ones I mean to say but if I stop talking, I'm afraid Roger will go away. "You can't wait to leave again." I am standing behind Roger who is organizing the items from his wallet on our bedroom bureau. I stand with one foot on top of the other and press down hard because sometimes I can actually hurt myself back into a calm place.

"Oh boy," Roger says and when he turns around, I quickly move my foot so I am on solid ground. "I'm a pilot," he says. "Whether I want to leave or not is moot."

"It's this place," I say.

"You think this place makes me want to leave?"

"I think it does if it means you could leave me," then I bite the inside of my cheek, which is still sore from this morning. It starts to bleed.

"I'm not going to respond to that, Mal. This should be a great time for you. You don't work. The Island has its own school. You drop the kids off and can go for a walk, go to the pool or the beach, learn to play golf, cook—you love to cook, for God's sake—it's gorgeous and safe here. What is the problem?"

"We don't belong here," I say. "We don't have any friends."

"We have friends here," he says, "all the parents at the School. I mean, they're not like our friends at home but they will be. We've only been here a month. You need to give it more time. Get to know the other mothers."

The other mothers wear jewelry to the Morning Announcements. Diamond rings and thick bangles made out of real gold. Chunky necklaces with large beautiful stones. They all glitter. Even their ponytails are perfect.

"How do I get to know them?" I ask. "They won't even talk to me." My friends in Cleveland, nearly all of us grew up together. We lived on the same set of streets. We all went to the same college. We never had to try to belong because we belonged to each other.

Finally Roger puts his arms around me and pulls me into his chest. "Listen, Babe, everything is going to work out fine. I promise."

"Why do you call me Babe?" And there it is, something coming out of my mouth that I think but do not want to say and Roger pushes me away. Roger never called me Babe until we came here. He called me Boo or Mallie. But I've heard the Island husbands call their wives Babe.

"I'm going for a run," he says.

I have to make dinner. I decide on Taco Bar. The girls love it and I imagine Roger doesn't care what he eats as long as it is ready by the time he is back from his run and has poured his glass of red wine. While the meat is browning, I chop lettuce, tomatoes, onions and olives into separate little bowls. I put the shredded cheddar into a large bowl and pour four glasses of milk. I have given up wine for a while because I want to lose some weight and it's easier to not drink than it is to not eat.

The seasoned browned meat tastes delicious but maybe I should just have salad. I'm not fat, exactly, but I still haven't lost all the baby weight I gained from Scarlett and compared to the other mothers, I feel too big. A little obese. "But you are thin," Isabella Torres had said the day at Morning Announcements when I complimented her on how great she looked and lamented my own flabby arms and pouching belly.

"Not like you," I had said, "you look like a teenager, really, you're so skinny, I just don't know how you do it, I mean how does someone our age have a body like yours, it's just like . . ." meaning to give a compliment but sounding like a teenager in trouble. Isabella gave me a look I couldn't interpret. I thought maybe Isabella didn't understand English as well as I thought so I put my palms up and pressed them close to each other, to act out what I was trying to say. Charades. Sounds like . . .

There was a smile attached to Isabella's face that was more quizzical than pleased so then I said "Skinny, skinny, you" in a forced Spanish accent that sounded so awful it made me feel sick. I wanted Isabella to like me. I had not planned to complain to Isabella about my weight; it's just what came out. I had come to school that morning thinking I would see if Isabella wanted to go for coffee, right then after Morning Announcements, because we have children the same age and Isabella seemed like the nicest one out of the bunch and my girlfriends at home and I used to go to the coffee shop every morning after dropping our kids off at school. But Isabella had acted as though she didn't understand me, had patted my shoulder and turned away. I am remembering this as I turn the stove off. I touch the burner even though I know it is still hot. I have to get in the golf cart and pick up the girls from school. Most people on the Island have Bentleys and Mercedes and Porsches. Last week we saw a Ferrari. But no one drives a car on the Island. My skin feels hot and itchy under my freckles. There is a blister forming on my palm.

At ten, Alexandra is my oldest child but she is Daddy's girl, and already on her way to surly teenage-dom. She eats because she has to, is sulky during meals, and returns to her room as soon as she puts her dish in the sink. I understand how hard it must be for Alexandra—a new school, new friends, a whole new way of trying to fit in—so I try to let her do whatever she wants to do at home, her safe place.

Sabrina is eight, chubbier and less pretty than her sisters, a reader. In many ways a typical middle child, prone to tantrums and fits of rage. I cuddle Sabrina as often as Sabrina will let me, which these days is pretty often.

Scarlett is our baby. She is four, cherubic, girly and bubbly, blessedly oblivious to the changes this move has brought. I am determined that she will not be spoiled.

"Are tacos fattening?" Alexandra wants to know.

"Nothing is fattening if you eat it in moderation," I say.

"What's moderation?"

"Just eat slowly and stop when you're full, honey," I explain. "And why are you asking that anyway? Since when are you worried about getting fat?"

"It's gross," Alexandra says. "Fat people are gross."

I look at Roger and communicate without words to say something but he just takes a bite of a taco and smiles at her.

"Alexandra," I say, and I hear my voice rising a bit even though it's not the way I feel. I love having dinner with my family. I feel calm.

"Ali," my daughter says defiantly. "My friends all call me Ali."

"Well, I'm your mother and here in our home, you're still Alexandra to me." And always will be, I think, my love for this child—my first child—indescribable. I reach out to touch her hair but Alexandra recoils. So I take a deep breath, remembering the pains of near adolescence, and wish I had poured myself a glass of the red wine Roger is drinking.

"Anyway, as I was saying, don't say mean things like that, honey."

"Mean things like what?"

"Like fat people are gross. Think about the people you love who might be a little overweight. Like Grandma."

And I should let that be that. I used to. But now, when Alexandra doesn't respond, I say, "And, anyway, you're not fat so I don't want to hear you saying things like that anymore, ok?"

"Fine," Alexandra says. "OK? Fine." She starts to tear up.

"Jeez, Babe," Roger says and when he reaches out to soothe our daughter, Alexandra puts her wet cheek on her father's hand and starts crying in earnest.

I pick up my fork but set it right back down. I look at Roger and raise my eyebrows and my shoulders to ask, *How did this happen?* Roger doesn't understand.

"You are yelling at them," he says.

"I am not," I say. I am surprised.

"Yes you are," Alexandra shouts. "You are. You always do. You're always yelling at me!"

"Cut the drama, Alexandra," I say with a sigh, "and finish your dinner." I am about to look at Roger and try again, to roll my eyes and convey our mutual exasperation when he pushes away from the table and stands up.

"Is it possible to have a pleasant dinner around here once in a while?" He picks up his wine and goes into his office.

My daughters and I continue eating in silence but I have to be careful because I am not really eating—I am poking the prongs of my fork into my tongue. This is exactly the kind of thing I have been talking about, or trying to talk about, with Roger but I never say it right. Roger is not happy at home anymore. I don't know what to do. I want to make him happy, make them all happy. It is my job.

"You made Daddy mad," Sabrina says. "You have to say sorry."

"You have to finish eating and go watch TV," I say, but I know Sabrina is right: this is what Roger and I tell the children to do when they misbehave. Own up. Take responsibility. Say you're sorry. But right now I think all of the apologies are owed to me because I didn't do anything wrong.

"You have to," Sabrina says.

"And I will," I say because I am the adult, the mother. "Now let's finish our dinner." When I go to stick my fork into my salad, I see blood on it.

The next morning, Roger accompanies me and the girls to Morning Announcements. I want this to make me feel safe but instead it makes me feel mad. He does not have to go back to work for three days but he is wearing his pilot's uniform anyway. He has Scarlett in his arms and two of the other mothers who never speak to me are standing on either side of him, cooing over my youngest child, a child they see every day and have never paid any attention to before.

I love Roger. He is the most wonderful man on earth. But he isn't handsome. He is short and beginning to bald but he has good features and keeps himself in great shape. Nearly all of the other Island School mothers are second wives, trophy wives, and their older husbands rarely make an appearance at school in the mornings.

"Why do you always have to flirt with those women?" I ask him when we are walking home.

"What women?" he asks.

"Mirabelle, Giselle, Lola's mother—I can't remember her name."

"They were playing with the baby," Roger says. "And Lola's mother's name is Ana. They're nice girls. You might try talking to them more."

"I've tried!" I say, in exasperation. "I try to talk to them in the mornings, at Morning Announcements, I . . ."

"Well, no wonder Bascomb thinks our kids can't behave. You're not supposed to talk at Morning Announcements."

I stop walking and it takes Roger about ten steps to realize I am no longer at his side. He turns around.

"Now what?"

"Are you scolding me? Telling me how to behave at the school? And how do you know Bascomb thinks our children can't behave?" My back is starting to ache. I want to sit down. Right here. On the ground.

"Because she called me," he says, and resumes walking. I catch up with him and pull on the back of his shirt.

"Hey," he says. "What is wrong with you?"

"Me? What is wrong with me? Why did Bascomb call you? *When* did she call you?"

"Keep your voice down, Mallory. Lord, what is the matter with you today?"

"What is the matter with *you*?" I shout, knowing it's childish but my head is spinning. I am so angry that I can't think.

"Jesus," Roger says.

"When did Bascomb call you?" I want to know.

"Yesterday. On my cell. I got the call just after we landed. She said you and the girls were very disruptive during Morning Announcements and that she needed everyone to follow the same rules, to be quiet and respectful while she gave the announcements."

"Me and the girls? Me? This is insane. Why didn't you tell me?"

"I'm telling you now." Roger starts walking again, more quickly now as if he is trying to get away from me and I have to jog a bit to catch up to him. Now the pain in my back is spurring me on.

"Why did she call you? I'm the one taking care of the girls, I'm the one who's home with them."

"I don't know. What happened anyway?"

"Oh my God," I say. "Nothing. That woman is ridiculous! The girls saw a plane in the sky and they thought it was you so they were saying hello to you and I was just trying to quiet them down when . . ."

This time, Roger stops in his tracks. "Look, Mal," he begins, "I don't know how to say this. We've been here a month now and we're going to be here at least ten more. I don't know what's happened to you, why you've changed so much."

"I haven't changed at all," I say. And I haven't. I know it. I wish I could change. If I could change, I think things would be different. Better. But I don't know how.

"You were never like this before."

"Like what?"

"So critical. You seem to hate everyone at the school, you mock them constantly and sometimes you're nasty and rude. Come on, we live here for Christ's sake."

These things are not true. Sure, I make fun of Eliza Barricelli's injected lips that make her look like a blowfish, and the wide range of fake breasts popping out of tanks and halters at 8:00 in the morning. I think it is absurd that so many of the other mothers get dressed up just to take their kids to school but I only say these things to Roger. They are jokes we are in on together. I don't hate everyone or anyone at the school. I'm never outwardly nasty or rude to any of them. If anything, I'm too nice and make a fool of myself. But the other mothers don't like me, and I know it, and mocking them with Roger helps me get through that. I want to tell him this but Roger has already begun walking again. I think he is afraid I will start yelling again, that I embarrass him here, so I keep quiet and follow slowly so I can feel the back pain with every step I take. I will figure out a way to bring this problem up later.

"Cook out? What is cook out?" Giselle Fiazzo's first language is Italian. Her second is French and her third is Spanish.

"Oh, a barbecue," I say. "At our house. Friday night. I'm hoping you and Roberto and your kids can come."

"Friday? Yes, ok, sure, we come. Not Roberto, he is in Milan but yes, we come."

"Great. See you at 6:00."

The cook out was Roger's idea, his response when I was finally able to explain the real problem: that The Island School mothers didn't like me, that they judged me, not the other way around. So Roger said why not clear the air, invite them all over, "show them our Midwestern hospitality."

He is away all week and actually isn't even going to get home until the party is underway but for the first time since we arrived here, I'm actually glad that he's not home. I need to show him that I can do this, that I am the same Mallie he dated all through college and married right after. I have imagined what the party will look like, what I will wear, how all our guests will be hanging out in our yard eating and drinking and having a great time.

I am excited. I love giving parties and I've always been good at it. All week I have been preparing. While the kids are in school, I leave the Island to shop for groceries, paper products. At Morning Announcements, some of the other mothers are actually smiling at me. I can't believe it. I wish I had thought of this before.

In my experience, if you lived somewhere you reached out to the new neighbors, tried to make them feel at home. But The Island has its own rules. Here the new person has to do the reaching out but that is fine. I can do it. I'm just happy and relieved to have finally figured it out. It is the best week I've had since we moved here.

I dig out my old recipes, find my serving platters and bowls, the big plastic tubs for beer. The anxiety that has plagued me disappears in the presence of the things that belong to me. Everyone on The Island has come from somewhere else and that is the key: you bring your customs and comforts into your new environment and it makes you happy, calms you down. You share what is your own. That is how you make your life here. You don't try to be like them to make them like you; you introduce yourself to them just exactly as you are.

Words are coming back to me. The inside of my mouth is healing. My thoughts are clear. I am saying what I mean to my children, to clerks at shops, to the other mothers when they ask if they can bring anything.

"No, no," I say, "nothing, really. I'm just so happy you are coming." And it's true. I am genuinely happy when they smile and I'm not looking beneath those smiles for what I think they really mean. I take them at their word.

It is so simple. The other mothers' affectations, their appearance, everything about them belongs to them just as much as my freckles and old sneakers and plaid kitchen curtains belong to me. Maybe they are insecure, too. Maybe they need to get dressed up and have their hair done and work out until they're ready to drop in order to feel good about themselves. It makes me feel sad for them because it is such hard work. I can barely pull a brush through my hair before piling the kids in the golf cart for school. I shouldn't have mocked them. I get it now.

When Roger comes home, I will hug him and thank him, tell him he was right and that I am sorry for having been so crazy. I will be a better wife from now on. I will stop trying to catch him in an affair I really don't think he's having. In all his years as a pilot, I had never thought that once until we got here. I feel sorry that I was so stupid. But I can fix that.

The girls are so excited about the party. Alexandra actually hugged me last night. I know she is also trying to fit into a new, strange environment. I will buy them all new outfits for the party. I will let Alexandra pick out her own new clothes.

I pick up the girls from school early so they can set up their toys and games on the patio before the party begins. Now they are having a snack in front of the TV and I am placing the small multi-colored tin buckets for mustard and ketchup on the tables. I have baskets of peanuts in their shells, blue and green paper plates, napkins and utensils, and little vases of white daisies. We've been to a couple of events on the Island and I know those parties were catered and professionally decorated but not only can we not afford such indulgences, I trust Roger's wisdom: nobody is better at being Midwestern than me.

My famous bratwursts are soaking in dark beer; my potato salad is ready in the fridge, garnished with hard boiled egg slices and paprika. Old school, the way my grandmother made it when I was growing up. Bottles of beer are on ice in the big plastic tubs and pitchers of lemonade are readied for the kids. Everything looks perfect. In Cleveland, every Friday in the summer, we'd have our friends over for burgers or hot dogs or kielbasa and beers. We'd eat and drink and later put the music on and dance on the lawn or play charades. I have put our speakers in the window facing the patio and small pads of paper and a coffee cup full of pens on the sill. I look at my decorated patio with great pride. This is going to be terrific.

At 6:00, I'm in my cut-off jean shorts, a "Cleveland Rocks" t-shirt and flip flops, standing near the front door waiting for my guests to arrive. Sabrina and Scarlett, in matching t-shirt and shorts outfits, are on the patio making sure all their toys and games are ready. Alexandra, in a peasant dress and sandals she selected, is sitting at one of the picnic tables. I painted her toenails a pale blue. She looks beautiful. Each child has a paper cup of lemonade. There are baskets of chips and pretzels and Cheetos out and as soon as everyone arrives, I will light the grill and start to cook my brats. It has been a long time since we have had them and I can't wait for the smell to take up all the air in the yard. Roger will be home around 7:00 and I am as excited to see him as I was on our wedding day, when we were getting ready to start our life together. This is a different kind of party but it is going to celebrate the same thing. We are starting our new life together.

"Mamma, where are they?" Sabrina is walking into the house. It is 6:45 and no one has arrived. She starts to cry.

"They'll be here soon, sweetie. Come here," I say, pulling her into a hug. But the truth is I am already beginning to feel a bit of Sabrina's panic. I did say this Friday, didn't I? 6:00, right? Why wasn't anyone here yet? Had they forgotten? No, no, I reminded everyone today at Morning Announcements. I am not going to make myself crazy. They will be here. Soon.

When it is 7:00, I can't deny my despair. Had something better come up? Did they just say yes but never intend to come? I don't know these people. Or maybe I do. Maybe they are the people I thought they were. Who am I kidding? Did Roger trick me into this? He should be home by now.

I feel the panic rising and have to do something. I decide to feed my kids. How will I explain this to them? That their house is all ready for a party and no one is coming. We are having our own party, I will tell them. Because we have food and drinks and music and we are a lot of fun. We are all we need. Daddy will be home soon. Any minute.

And he will think I screwed this up, that this is all my fault.

But then there is a knock on the door and when I open it, two of the families are standing on my front porch.

"Miami time!" Mirabelle Perez calls out. "We are never on time!" I've heard about it, Miami time—the antithesis of Midwestern punctuality—but I smile in relief. I open the door wide to let my guests in.

The mothers are wearing designer sundresses and stylish hats and high-heeled strappy sandals that I think will sink into my lawn, the children all in clothes I've seen in magazines. But I am relieved that Alexandra is wearing something that looks similar and that she loves. I watch these two mothers giving me the once over but I am happy again. I am not going down.

"Welcome to Ohio," I say, but I can see no one gets the joke. "This is a cook out and I'm in cook out clothes." The explanation does not help and I vow, despite my reclaimed happiness, that I will not talk too much this evening.

"Hola!" Mirabelle kisses me on both cheeks and hands me a big white box. "This cake from Aluro's, to die for," she says, walking past me toward the patio, followed by her nanny and her three little children. "Oh, look out there, so cute."

"Yes, so cute out there," Giselle says, ushering in her own two children and their nanny and carrying a white plastic bag. Behind her is a man in a chauffeur's uniform holding what looks like a case of wine. "Go, go, follow the Mrs. Perez nanny, go," Giselle says to her children, and then to me, "yes, is so cute here. You do it yourself, no? And here," she points to her chauffeur, "we bring you this wine, is from my family's vineyard in Italy."

I am holding the cake. I motion to the chauffeur to follow me into the kitchen. But just as I am turning, another guest arrives. An older woman, stunning, in white linen pants and a pale blue silk tank. Her neck is draped in strands of enormous pearls. I have never seen her before.

"Bonjour," the woman says, and tries to put the bottle of wine she is carrying into my already full arms. "Ah, no matter," she says, and takes the wine with her as she walks through the house.

At home, something like this—a stranger at my door, clearly coming to the party but having no idea she is being greeted by the hostess—would not have bothered me at all. In fact, I would have introduced myself and welcomed the stranger warmly. But as I watch this woman move fluidly through my living room toward my patio door, my euphoria dips a bit in the recollection that I am still very new to this Island and that my old customs might not always be able to serve me. Giselle's chauffeur is still standing there waiting for instructions so I says *vamanos* and lead him to the kitchen, just at that moment thinking he might be Italian. I barely know Spanish. I do not know Italian.

No more words. Too much trouble. I motion for him to put the wine on the counter. From my kitchen window, I watch my party beginning to form. I had only planned on beer and lemonade and wonder how my guests will react to drinking wine from paper cups.

I open the cake box to an elaborate confection topped with cherries soaked in some kind of liqueur I can smell and ground nuts pressed perfectly into the icing all around it. I didn't buy dessert plates or forks because I spent two days baking giant Snickerdoodles and Black & White Cookies that I thought everyone would just eat with their hands. Am I supposed to make coffee? I close the box and decide to think about the cake later. I go outside to the grill.

Now it's 7:30 and our party is in full swing. There are around thirty adults, only a handful of fathers, and sixteen kids. I watch them and think everyone is having fun. The men are drinking the beers, the women seem fine sipping wine out of the paper cups, the nannies—who I wasn't expecting but am just fine with having—are playing with the kids. And I am busy grilling, putting the crispy brats and hot dogs for the kids into buttered buns on the platter, then running into the kitchen to get the potato salad, the cole slaw, pulling the sweet baked beans topped with bacon, brown sugar and ketchup out of the oven and taking everything to the buffet. It smells fantastic. No one has offered to help but I can't fault them for that—these are my guests. They are also people who are not used to cooking or serving. But no one seems to notice me, how hard I am working, no one comes up to chat with me while I'm at the grill. But it's fine. It's all fine. I am determined to be patient, to watch and learn. This is not Cleveland, these are not my old friends who would have been clustered around me, refilling my beer, and taking the readied food off the grill and to the table for me. But it's fine.

The food is on the table. I go into the kitchen to wash my hands. It is a mess. The other mothers all have housekeepers and I wish I had one now, just someone who could help me clean this up so I can join my party. But I look out the window and everyone seems to be enjoying themselves so I quickly clean up.

When I get outside, I see that no one is eating, except for the kids munching on chips and drinking lemonade. I'm wondering if I could find the silver bell my mother bought me last Christmas and if ringing it to announce dinner is a good idea when I feel someone tap me on the shoulder.

"The door was open so I let myself in." I turn around to see Mrs. Bascomb standing behind me, a bottle of champagne in her hand.

When school first started, I felt sorry for Mrs. Bascomb. I could tell she had been pretty when she was younger but the years had tightened and wrinkled her and in this community of extraordinarily beautiful people, it is impossible to look at a woman without seeing what you are not. I had wanted to befriend the Headmistress, perhaps even join forces to determine how best to survive on this surreal private residential island that had its own school. I thought Mrs. Bascomb would appreciate me, my unpretentiousness, that I wore nylon gym shorts and t-shirts and sneakers to Morning Announcements instead of designer loungewear. But from the start, every time I tried to talk with Mrs. Bascomb privately, I had the feeling the Headmistress didn't like me, that she was purposely distracted by almost anything that she could use to excuse herself and move away. And just last week, Mrs. Bascomb had actually scolded me. In front of everyone. And called Roger. She doesn't like me. I am not imagining this.

Bascomb has a new haircut, the third one I've seen since school started and that was just a month ago. She is so obviously trying to be one of these women who live here but clearly she is not. She must know that. They do. I do. I think it is pathetic that she is so vain but I won't tell Roger even though I do not feel bad mocking her in my head. She deserves it. She is wearing a long blue cotton skirt, a white linen button down blouse, a red blazer and some nautical scarf around her neck. She looks like she's about to board the stranded yacht on Gilligan's Island. I smile at my joke and my face matches my greeting.

"Mrs. Bascomb, how nice of you to come," I say.

"Here," Mrs. Bascomb says, pushing the champagne toward me. "It's chilled."

"Thank you," I say, taking the bottle and the high road, though thinking that at least in my own home the Headmistress might be polite to me. And I'm wondering who invited her to my cook out. Bascomb doesn't seem to notice anything out of place; she is not embarrassed about being at a party I did not invite her to.

Maybe everyone at the School invites the Headmistress to their parties. Maybe you are supposed to, or maybe the Headmistress just knows to show up anytime any of the school families are having an event. There is a lot to learn. But whatever the reason for Bascomb being here, I am committed to being a gracious hostess, so I say, "Would you like a glass of champagne?"

"Doesn't look like you have any glasses, my dear," Bascomb says, surveying the buffet and the table where I've set up the drinks. "Well, when in Rome . . ." and she retrieves the bottle from my hand and heads toward the paper cups.

It's ok, it's ok, it's ok, I chant to myself. But when Bascomb has her cup of champagne, she joins a group of moms and I hear Lorena Schuler exclaim, "Tricia! How lovely. I didn't know you were going to be here."

Neither did I. And how the hell is Lorena, also new to the Island, on a first name basis with Bascomb, who has never once told me to call her Tricia. I let the anger in now because it feels good to be mad about this. Where the hell is Roger? It is after 8:00. And I don't know what I'm supposed to do. Go join my guests? Get a plate and start eating so they will eat? Go up to my room and take a nap?

I choose the buffet. My teeth hurt and need something to chomp down on. I pick up a plate and begin to fill it with my homemade cook out fare. Then I walk toward another group of mothers and squeeze my way in.

"Dinner's on," I say, "please. Go help yourselves."

The mothers are looking down on my plate. Then two of them look over my shoulder at the buffet.

"How . . . rustic. Where did you find a caterer who could do this kind of thing for you?" Elizabeth Treat asks.

"Oh, I cooked this all myself," I say, wondering how Elizabeth could have missed me standing at the grill.

"Really? That is quite sweet," Elizabeth says. "Looks good...very good, yes . . . but we ate before we came."

"You ate before coming to a cook out?" I say, with a little laugh meant only as surprise but clearly Elizabeth takes it another way.

"Yes, we always do. It's not personal, just what we do, because of they way we eat." The other mothers in this circle begin to nod their heads as if they, too, have eaten before they came because it is just what they do and then Elizabeth turns her back to me.

Oh no. No, no, no. I'm sorry but this is not happening. This is my house. I suck in my bottom lip, clamp it between my teeth. I have to do something. I have to say something. She has to turn around.

"Oh, I'm sorry, I'm so sorry, really," I say, "I didn't know, I could have made something else, something you'd like, if I'd known, I would have . . ." I am fumbling, stumbling, moving the full plate of food I am now feeling embarrassed to have made, to be about to eat, in my hands in awkward gestures meant to support my apology and even though it's not what I thought I was going to say, it's working. Elizabeth turns back around and smiles at me. Just when I think I have said the right thing, she pats me on the shoulder and says, "Not to worry, dear. Enjoy your dinner."

I feel my face and neck fill with the kind of heat I know is settling into my freckles, making them turn blotchy and dark red. I am sick to my stomach.

I have to move so I walk away and take a seat at one of the tables. Just then, Giselle sits down next to me and from under the chair, pulls out her white plastic bag. Inside is an undressed salad from the Island Market.

"You brought your own dinner," I observe weakly.

"Of course, I do this always, everyone knows this," Giselle says. "is nothing personal."

I did not know this and is everything personal. Is a slap in the face. And now it is nearly 9:00 and Roger still hasn't showed up. Probably in a hotel screwing Ellie B. I should have known that. No wonder he wanted me to throw this party. No wonder he wants me to make friends—that would give him plenty of time to have his affair.

I want to leave. I want to go home. But I live here. I am at a party where I don't know anyone but everyone is my guest. And having a fine time. Look at them. They're completely comfortable, having drinks and chatting and laughing with each other. A couple of the husbands are standing up with brats in their hands but I am the only person sitting down with a plate of the food I cooked. I am going to eat it.

"Rogere!" I pick up the plastic fork and stab it into the potato salad when I hear that French woman's voice. "Mon cher, where have you been?" I look up and see Roger, in his pilot's uniform, walking onto the patio. Finally. I put the fork down. I am furious. I dig my nails into my thighs because I need to calm down. Roger is here. He's a pilot. Things happen. He didn't even call. But he's here now. All right. Good. I watch him hug that French woman and start to think it's a nice greeting until I remember that I have no idea who she is or how he knows her. I watch him shake hands with the men, air kiss the mothers in the circle around him. If he wasn't my husband in a uniform I have taken to and picked up from the dry cleaner a thousand times, I would wonder who the hell he was.

I take my hands off my thighs knowing there are dark blue half-moon marks in my skin. I am going to join Roger in that circle. It's where I belong. I'm about to get up when a cluster of mothers in front of my view part and there is Ellie B.

"Who is this vision?" the French woman says, embracing Ellie whom she clearly has never met. "Is this your wife? Our hostess?" Ellie B is also in her pilot's uniform. Her long dark hair is down and falls in a straight silky line down her back. She is smiling. She looks beautiful.

"No, not my wife. My partner in crime," Roger says, "Captain Ellie B. Ellie, this is Francoise Marcheline."

I watch this scene unfold. I am just staring at my husband, watching him perform some elaborate story. The children have begun playing a game and their voices make it impossible now for me to hear what he is saying so I focus on his movements, try to interpret his gestures, a party game I know. Roger's hands move up and down. Dropping? Flying? Falling from the sky? He points to Ellie and Ellie puts her hands over her ears, then over her eyes. Hear no evil. See no evil. I watch the crowd around them, their faces breaking into smiles, their mouths moving. I don't know what any of them are saying.

Someone's husband brings Roger a beer. I watch him drink deeply and then begin to look around, a gesture I recognize, think I understand.

"Over here, honey," I say. I have to be nice. It's what defines me, separates me from all of these strangers on my lawn. I stand up and walk toward my husband. I don't know this Francoise Marcheline who calls my husband Rogere or how he knows her. I don't know why he brought Ellie B to our party. But suddenly all I feel is relief because he is looking for me.

"Where's the bar, Babe?" he asks, before or instead of saying hello. I walk right up to him and he gives my shoulder a squeeze and kisses me on my forehead. Like you would a child.

Ok, I think. OK. It's all ok. If we were in Cleveland and this happened, I wouldn't think twice about it. I resurrect the small amount of party hope I have left and let it guide me.

"The bar? It's over there, honey. We have beer…and some wine, Mrs. Bascomb brought a bottle of champagne . . ."

"Hey Mal," Ellie says, and then in a fake whiny childlike voice that even my own children don't use when they want something, "the Captain promised me vodka."

"And vodka you shall have." Roger walks into the house.

You shall have? I follow him into the house.

"Roger?" I say, all hope now dissolved, the slow burn rising. "Um, hello? Why is Ellie B here? And why are you so late?"

"We had a really rough flight back, got in late. And Ellie hadn't eaten so I just invited her over. No big deal. She's our friend. Why didn't you set up a bar, Babe?" He is pulling three half empty bottles of vodka out of our liquor cabinet.

"Why didn't you call?' I say.

"Do we have tonic? Or soda water?"

"Roger," I try again, and then louder, "Roger!!"

"What? Jesus, Mallory, what is it?"

"What is it?"

"What's the problem? You're having a party. Why didn't you set up a bar?"

I'm thinking, *what about what I did do?* but I say, "I made brats so we're serving beer. And what do you mean *I'm* having a party? What are you, a guest here?"

"Oh boy," Roger says, shaking his head. "You really are something, Mal." He grabs the three vodka bottles and some tonic he finds in the cupboard and heads back outside.

"Roger!!" I want to follow him but I cannot move.

"Mallory, Jesus, keep it down. What is the matter with you?" He turns around to face me. "I don't know what else to say to you now and there's a ton of people on the patio. Lighten up. Try to have some fun."

From the kitchen window, I watch Roger set the vodka and tonic on the table with the beer and wine and lemonade, and what's left of Bascomb's champagne. He has made a bar. I watch him fix a vodka and tonic for Ellie B and I watch him hand it to her. All the lovely people gather around them again. I watch them having some fun. Without trying. I feel dizzy but determined. I go outside.

I want Roger to introduce me to Francoise Marcheline, as his wife, so I place myself in the circle next to my husband and look at him but he doesn't see me because Ellie is in the middle of a story about their flight home from Brazil and Roger begins the up and down gestures again, acting out the turbulence. The story is endless and repetitive but no one, except me, seems to mind. And then there are more stories, other people's stories of turbulent flights, scares, frights, bad airline food. People slip away and return with more drinks, Roger makes Ellie another vodka and tonic, I stand in my spot, my hands in the pockets of my cut-off shorts. I pinch the skin beneath the denim, which has gone soft and comforting from so many washes. My stomach is tied up in knots but it is also rumbling, like it's waiting for something to happen.

I stand there for hours, the words and gasps and laughter whizzing through my head. I have to pee but I don't dare move because I am standing watch and don't know what could happen if I were gone. At midnight, the Island siren sounds as it does at this time every night, but no one is making a move to leave. This is the sign of a successful party—no one wants to go home. Except the hostess. I take it as a sign.

I back out of the group but the truth is I could take all my clothes off and cartwheel my way away and no one would notice. My anger rose then fell like the flight Roger and Ellie could not stop talking about, but now it has just landed with a hard thump inside of me. And like all good crashed wreckage, it is on fire. As far as I am concerned, this party is over.

And other important things may be over, too, but first things first. Empty plates and cups are all over the buffet, on the drink table, tossed on the lawn as if the grass was a garbage dump, even though there is a huge trash can at the end of the table. I know these people are not used to cleaning up after themselves but this is ridiculous. I place an open paper bag on the lawn and squat down. Pain shoots through my knees and the pressure in my bladder has reached its limit. I take a good deep breath and begin to put the debris inside the bag.

Out of the corner of my eye, I see someone coming toward me. I think it might be someone coming to say thank you and, finally, good night. Exhausted, I rise, clutching the trash bag in one hand and wiping the other on my cut-off shorts. I have the smallest amount of gracious hostess left. Just enough to say goodnight.

"Yes, here you go," Francoise Marcheline says to me, and she puts something into my free hand. "Bathroom?"

It is a napkin. One she has used. I see traces of her dark lipstick and something else, something that is obviously food she has discarded from her mouth. I look up at the woman who just put a dirty napkin into my hand, whose spit is in my palm, and see that woman looking at me with impatience because I have not answered her question. Francoise Marcheline misinterprets my silence for lack of understanding and says, "le salle de bain? Bathroom? Bano?"

I understand perfectly: Francoise Marcheline thinks I am the maid. I drop the dirty napkin and the trash bag onto the grass and point to the house.

Against much loud protestation, I tell my three kids it is time for bed. The pretense is that I am a good mother, something that has never been a pretense before, and small children should be in bed at this hour but the truth is I have to get out of here and have nowhere else to go. I know my girls are having fun and want to stay up and that I should let them because no one else seems to think it is past time for little children to be put in bed but I can no longer bear being on the patio with these people who have no idea I am there, with my husband and his co-pilot holding court in the center of a group of people who are supposed to be talking to me, with other people's children playing with my children's toys, leaving half-eaten hot dog buns and cookie crumbs and peanut shells all over my patio. That I will have to clean up because I don't have a housekeeper or a nanny or a husband who will help. Because I am the maid.

Someone had found the rum cake and brought it out to the buffet and it is the only item that has completely disappeared, except for the cookies which the kids and nannies devoured. I do not understand why the other mothers won't touch potato salad but think nothing of eating fat pieces of sugary cake with their hands. I gather my daughters and take them upstairs. I send them all into Alexandra's room so I can go to the bathroom.

"I'll be right back," I say and close the door. Alexandra is saying something to me but I don't hear it.

It takes me a long time to pee because I have had to pee for so long. There are razor blades beneath the sink. I've cut myself before, just once, but it didn't hurt enough so I never did it again. And the blood made such a huge mess and, frankly, tonight I will have more than enough mess to clean up. These people are not worth my feelings. They are not worth my hurting myself. They are not worth anything. Not even Roger. He has become one of those people.

I go back to Alexandra's room.

"I can't believe you," she says, "this is the first time I was having any fun since we moved here. No one else has to go to bed."

"That's right," I say. I feel better. I have made myself feel better and I am agreeable.

"You are so mean," Alexandra says. "The meanest."

Say whatever you want, Alexandra. Nothing you say can hurt me now because I feel better. I bite my cheeks and dig my nails into the softest parts of my skin just to make sure and then I discover that I can't feel anything. Even better. So go ahead, honey. Say whatever you need to say.

I am hot, though. That I can feel. My bangs are damp and clinging to my forehead. Even though I am letting Alexandra carry on with her insults, what she is saying is not at all true. I am not mean. I am nice, thoughtful. Everyone I know has always said so. And I worked tirelessly to throw this party that everyone is having such a good time at. So, no, I am not mean. But I am hot. I am tired. And all of a sudden, I am hungry. Very hungry. I am mad with hunger. My shorts feel too tight at the waist and they're wet from sweat, sticking to the back of my thighs. I want to put my nightgown on. I want a glass of wine, a huge glass of Giselle's family's fancy red wine. I want some food.

"Stay in this room," I say to my children, not knowing if they will or not.

"Where are you going?" Alexandra screams.

"To a party."

I take a plate from the buffet, fill it with a brat and all the sides. I grab a full bottle of wine. Plate in one hand, bottle in the other, I go inside and back upstairs. In my room, I take my clothes off and put on my nightgown and get into bed with my plate and the wine.

My food is good. Really good, just the way I remember it, even though it has been sitting outside for hours. I take a big drink of the wine, right out of the bottle. It is too dry and it is bitter but I take a second swig anyway. It is terrible wine. Who drinks wine with bratwursts and baked beans?

Then I hear Alexandra screaming for me from her bedroom. She is calling me Mother and I wonder when that started. Mother. I don't even call my own mother Mother. I put the half eaten plate on the bed and go to see my children.

"I hate you," Alexandra says when I walk into the room. Sabrina and Scarlett are practically asleep on the floor. "You are totally unfair," Alexandra says. "None of the other moms are doing this!"

"Well, I am not the other mothers. Isn't that obvious to you by now? It certainly is to me." I tell Sabrina to go to her room. Then I lift Scarlett and follow her. "I'll be back," I say to Alexandra.

"I hate you," Alexandra says, again. She is crying.

"What are you crying about?" I ask her. "You had a fine time tonight. Stop the crying. I'll be back."

I put Sabrina and Scarlett in their beds. Their faces aren't washed, their teeth aren't brushed, they are still in their clothes. I am not a good mother. I turn out the light and close the door.

On my way back to Alexandra, I stop in my room and have a few more big bites of my food, a few more big sips of the bad wine, another bite of my food. My grandmother would be proud of me—the potato salad tastes just like her own. I am still chewing it, wiping drips from my chin back into my mouth, when I return to Alexandra.

"Did you hear what I said," Alexandra asks, as if there has not been a reprieve. "I hate you."

"Go to sleep," I say, and I am not kidding. I am famished now. I need to go back and eat.

"I have to put my nightgown on."

"No you don't. You can sleep in that dress."

"You have your nightgown on," Alexandra says defiantly.

"Yes, I do. But you look pretty in your new dress. Now get under the covers." I walk toward her.

"You're so stupid," Alexandra says. I know she is confused, maybe even a little scared, but I can't care about that now. She really needs to go to sleep. "You have mustard on your face."

"That's because I am eating," I say, shaking my head as if she should know this, "a brat with lots of spicy mustard. Did you have one?" The bad red wine is burning in my chest. I like it.

"That food is gross," Alexandra is sobbing in earnest now.

Tomorrow I will make this all right. I know Alexandra is unhappy but I know she is also tired. I just can't help her now. But I will help her tomorrow. Everything will be fine tomorrow. I walk over to the bed, thinking I am going to give Alexandra a hug and tuck her in. No more words.

"You're gross. You have food on your face and you're fat. You're so fat, it's disgusting!"

Then my daughter goes flying out of her bed. Because I slapped her that hard.

On the floor, Alexandra starts screaming.

"Shut up," I say, in a quiet, controlled voice, my Mommy voice that has miraculously returned to me. What a relief. "Get back in bed," I say, as if Alexandra has gotten out of bed on purpose.

"I want Daddy," Alexandra sobs.

"Your Daddy's busy with his girlfriend so good luck with that," I say. I close the door without knowing if my daughter is back in bed or not. Or if she is seriously hurt. If I wanted to, I could go into Alexandra's room right now and hug all this nonsense away. But I don't want to. I want to finish my dinner.

I shove a forkful of cold beans into my mouth, take too big a bite of the bratwurst in the soggy bun. Mustard shoots out and lands on my lap. I lift it off with my finger and rub it into the comforter. I slapped Alexandra. The mayonnaise in the cole slaw may be curdled but I swallow a sour forkful anyway. I take three long gulps of the awful red wine. I wonder who would drink this wine and think it is good and then realize that no one would. People would say it was good because Giselle brought it, because she is rich and beautiful and it is from her family's vineyard in Italy. But no one could think it was good. And then I know that Giselle brought it to me because no one else with any taste would drink it. That is who she thinks I am.

I wipe up the remaining sauce from the beans with the last bite of the bratwurst roll and put it in my mouth. I want more. I actually slapped Alexandra right out of her bed. I didn't know I had the power. I am a mother who would sooner throw herself off a cliff than hurt her children but that woman was not here tonight to save Alexandra from this one. The other mother.

Acknowledgments

"Beloved Child," previously published in *Keeping the Wolves at Bay,* Autumn House Press, 2010.

All love and thanks to Alice Elliot Dark, Kathie Klarreich and Laurel Yulish; and to my family: Dad, Mom & Alex, Lee & Regina & Jack, Krissy, and Jenny & Steve.

The Autumn House Fiction Series

*Winners of the Autumn House Fiction Prize

Design and Production

Cover and text design by Chiquita Babb

Cover photograph: iStockphoto

Author photograph: Maureen Davis

Text set in Centaur fonts, designed by Bruce Rogers in 1914, with a complementary italic font (originally titled Arrighi) designed by Frederic Warde in 1925; display text set in Lilith fonts, designed by David Rakowski in 1992

Printed by McNaughton & Gunn on 55# Glatfelter Natural